THE UNHEARD OF BARCALDINE

ASH BANSS

Contents

Contents

Memories never die; they haunt

CHAPTER ONE

The air felt cool as it breezed through the woods of Lanthom Cove. The stagnant chill left over the town added to the wrath of unending rains. It was now well understood that the skies of Lanthom cove could never be correctly predicted. And yet, this ever-changing behaviour never bothered anyone, at least not anymore. Maybe they were just habitual now. After all habit is what saves you when everything else fails in life, and the world of Lanthom Cove wasn't very different either. It was very much like ours, with minor differences in the horrors it had seen.

It was rarely sunny during this time of the year and the shadows from the sky kept a close watch at all times. Despite the constant chaos, Lanthom Cove never failed to carry its everyday course. If ever questioned, and contrary to what one might expect, its residents always remarked their life as likeably aloof. Was it because theirs was the only human settlement at a stretch of unending miles anywhere from the town's borders? False pride maybe.

But nevertheless, this remoteness offered a visual treat of green terrain all around. One could fairly mark that it was a composed, familiar, and a functional town. But even then, under its shadow, something was breeding imperceptibly, hiding and silent, and therefore not immediately apparent. Like they say, evil has its mark everywhere, and Lanthom Cove was no different – it had one such exception and that had its own story to tell.

The wind was turbulent around the house. It always seemed so even when the wind was still everywhere else in the town. The window dangling at the weak support of the loose hinges fluttered dreamily and had been the same for almost three consecutive nights in a row. This added to the deterioration of that weary house, standing rigidly for almost sixty-five plus years now, and like I earlier said, silent and watchful of every passing decade. The house retained its old-world charm. It was a typical big mansion, once owned by a wealthy British family during the World War, but later was disowned and sold. Reason? Completely forgotten.

The structure reflected its vintage character and its occupant eeriness whispered all day, and yet was audible to no one. The house had a past, one that was speculated by numerous spectators, only to ultimately vanish into the grit of a distant time. In the end what continued to live was the house, all alone, to be the only bearer of some gruesome memories and the last witness of its veracious truth.

It's true that the memories of the mansion had become rusty and couldn't even survive in the minds of a few, only to be later carried through the words of passing generations. Yet, whosoever saw the house, closely, felt that the brick walls were hiding something inside, or was it someone, guarding it for years now, and which in return watched the world with a pair of sinister eyes.

Those eyes even had a voice, which was better left unheard, for good, even though; it longed to be heard. The manor well carried its age. The old architecture, the dying wood, and the broken panes, all put together marked its wrinkled state. Even the passing brush of air smelt stale after touching the vicinity of this gothic-looking mansion;

its venom still stung hard. The wood that once shone was now left with an ugly lacklustre colour, and the slender pillars, which in their crowing era supported the large porch, were now stationed naked with their skin chipped off decades ago.

Clocks had ticked to millions of hours yet not a foot had stepped inside Barcaldine to solace its tearing beauty. On the contrary, stating this would be a lie, because once someone did break-in through the forbidden, and then the consequences were witnessed by the whole town.

The house faced a deep blue river and stood before a forest woven so skilfully that it almost appeared to be mansion's very own throne. From above, the close gathering of trees seemed like a long thick arm wrapped around the house in comfort. Four more houses ran along the same lane on its either side and yet it felt the house had no neighbours who could hear if something went inside it. It was the house of mystery, roaring in its silent voice, speaking in a muffled language, waiting to be heard.

The view was wraithlike yet fascinating. It stood distinct from any other house of its time. This was, as once famously known, the *Barcaldine House*.

CHAPTER TWO

For Martha Bates, life never seemed easy. All the way from her childhood to high school, from personal life to career, she found it tough, making through all of it. But it wasn't because her life was in truth difficult, but the passions and temper of youth often clashed with the people and situations around her. A mother whose concern for Martha's best interest was often miscalculated as intrusion and that made her seem difficult to her only child. But now, at thirty-nine years of age and a mother of two herself – Ben; ten and Susan; twelve – Martha could now reflect on her past more with logic than fervour, able to see people, and their actions, for what they were, and not how it affected her intentions.

That same rigor once added immensely to her vibrancy. She was one of those women whose beauty lay in their conduct rather than in the confinement of their facial lines. Gifted with a lean body and eyes to die for, Martha carried herself with sufficient grace, to be able to walk in any room, and grab every man's attention, and even women on some occasions. Her unforgettable face also carried innocence. Well, that was exactly what took David Edment to fall in love with her, thus binding them into a marriage of fifteen years.

It all started when Martha met David during the initial days of her career. She was a law graduate, but unfortunately getting a desired job wasn't as easy as she conferred it to be. Lack of experience marked her rejection everywhere she applied. It took some hard work to secure a beginner's but comfortable position in a law firm. This marked the beginning of a new ride. It was during this time that she met David, a senior lawyer then, and later married him after two years. She worked for another year and then left the job after Susan was born. With a burgeoning desire to start a family, she agreed without much apprehensions. It surprised her how the track of her life, that was once centred around a burning desire to be a career woman, changed into one of quiet settlement in the suburbs. Martha Edment now lived a settled life with her family and she finally felt the peace that she had been chasing all her life.

After a childhood spent in a small town, Martha aspired travelling to big glittery cities. New York came as an answer. She moved there when only eighteen for higher education. She learnt a lot just by being in the city alone. Martha now felt a belonging to New York as if she had never lived anywhere else, especially after spending crucial years of growing up as a woman under its shade, and with that her small-town memories grew distant. Even though her parents insisted and pulled her hard to make a return, nothing could persuade this woman of convictions to go back to her roots. Occasionally, she would pay her visits, but they were always as short as she could manage to keep them. Though her perspective took an unexpected turn when she entered family life. It made her realize how much she meant to her parents. From there on, Martha's visits were more out of gratitude than obligation.

Everything was going fine, until now. David had lost his job leaving him unemployed with persisting financial crisis. Their house came with a hefty monthly instalment to pay off the huge loan David had taken a few years ago and as of his involuntary termination six months ago, their financial position had turned bleak.

Things were becoming difficult as the days passed by. It was eleven in the night and the rain struck heavily outside. Ben and Susan were deep asleep.

"We are not going make it," said David as he lay on his bed with his wife beside him.

"Don't say that, David. We will make it, we just have to keep going for now," Martha replied reassuringly.

David was naturally broken after months of efforts in looking for a new job and it was only human to sound hopeless. But he also knew it was time to tell Martha the hard bit and he blurted it as quickly as possible.

"We have to leave this house soon. The notice of eviction has been issued."

Martha raised her head swiftly. The horror and shock in her eyes quickly melted into tears of pain and defeat. She knew they were behind instalments for quite a few months now. The bank's faith in them had become shaky, but she had never thought that the eviction could happen so soon. She blankly looked at the wall, as if someone had sucked life out of her body. Tears rolled down quietly, and the only thing she managed to say was. "Where will we go?!"

David turned and looked at her. He eyed her briefly and silently. It pained him to see her broken, but he knew he had to have the difficult conversation in order to answer the question Martha had asked.

"Martha, we can't afford all this anymore, the city life is too costly for us now."

Martha raised her head in a quick lift as if his last statement was intended to be challenging to her. She quickly snapped out of that brief moment of grief and caught the words that mattered, that were spoken exactly how David had intended them to be, and this time she questioned demandingly.

"What did you mean by city life?"

Martha behaved ignorant even though he had stated his mind very explicitly. Her eyes narrowed with a guarding vicious look towards his last statement. David remained silent, keeping his eyes low. A deep stillness took over the room. The turmoil going outside began to congest their ears and Martha sensed what was coming. She asked again.

"What do you mean by that?!" The silence broke and she was unapologetically loud this time.

David raised his head and looked into her eyes deeply, keeping the answer still locked inside his hardened throat. He could merely nod his head and Martha instantly realized what had happened. Not even in her wildest dreams she had expected this. Bad days come and people recover; she believed the same story when it came to her. But unfortunately, the usual tale seemed to have had missed her call. Tears rolled down her cheeks as she spoke further.

"No! We can't leave New York, David. This is our home! This is where we belong, God dammit!"

She could not imagine leaving New York. It was a part of her sense of existence now. In a matter of minutes, Martha grew repulsively painful to convince. "We don't have an option, Martha," said David trying to calm his already grieving wife.

"But where will we go?!" Martha snapped back. "Leaving this house is already too much to bear, David. But I understand that it is not in our hands anymore. And now you are asking me to leave New York too?" She then looked straight at him and added almost feeling broken, "I don't think I would be able to take that." He grew silent as if her confession failed him to contest any further.

After all, she had demanded an answer to the most valid question, *where will they go?* Conflicting with what Martha perceived, it was not his inability to provide an appropriate answer, but a preparatory silence towards announcing the next piece of news. David had it in mind for days but waited patiently for a suitable moment, and this was it.

"I have a place where we can go," he revealed in a rush.

"What?" Martha was wiping her cheek with the back of her palm and restrained it mid-way.

"Yes. My father left a property in his will under my name – a house. It has been in the family for a while now. I know I have never mentioned it before, never thought it would hold any significance in our lives, but, yes, I own that property."

She crunched her eyes in confusion. Contrary to what David had assumed, getting accustomed to these new developments wasn't that easy for Martha.

"What? Where is it?" she finally questioned failing to contest any further. Her nose made sniffing sounds every time she drew words out of her mouth.

"It's in a town called Lanthom Cove." It thundered outside as he spoke. The rain grew harsher as he continued. "It is at a four hours' of drive from New York. I have been to that place once, but long ago. It's a beautiful house Martha; I know you will love it."

He was almost pleading now for Martha to consider this. Martha gave a look of disagreement and sighed away agitatedly towards the window, away from his imploring eyes. She got up and went near the open window. It was raining heavily. As she stood there, sprinkles of water brushed her burning cheeks. She was unable to find a way of accepting the fact of leaving New York.

"Honey, please, we have no other choice. Don't be like this."

He went closer to her, turned her face to his and held her in his arms. "Trust me, keep faith in me, you will love the house," he said convincingly gazing into her eyes deeply, trying to reassure that everything would turn out just fine as it used to be. "Just support me in this major leap, Martha; it isn't easy for me either."

A blow of cool air hauled in through the window square, lugging with it the rejuvenated smell of fresh earth. Her skin felt jitters of cold and Martha leaned forward over David's chest. It was a necessary leap, but to Martha it seemed like a compulsion. An unknown land, a place that her instincts do not recognize at all would be her new home. An alien feeling emerged and froze vaguely somewhere beneath her heavy heart, whispering to her that the transition would not be fruitful. *Will I ever come back to New York?*

Only if that feeling was a bit more coherent, she would have had explained it to David. After another debate that almost broke into a quarrel again, she agreed reasonably to the facts that David pointed at and understood that her continued attachment to a place could not sustain her family. Martha finally sacrificed her will and agreed to move to her new house that might become her truth for the rest of her life.

But Martha still could have had said *no*, only if she knew what awaited her, *only if*.

CHAPTER THREE

The news came as a surprise to Ben, but then he was too young to understand the reasons behind this abrupt change. Even so, like his mother, he didn't appear very thrilled about the decision. On the other hand, Susan was full of protests, but that couldn't alter the course of the events either. It took David and Martha ten days to complete the tiresome work of wrapping up the house. The eleventh day they were ready to head for their new home, which was an unknown territory to all of them. David made the required arrangements to transfer the heavy load.

They were about to leave the house. Martha stood near the car holding an umbrella, counting her final minutes with the house after which she was to be driven away from the city she loved the most. In that moment, it was only natural to ruminate about all those memories that made this house so dear and special to her. It felt no less than letting go of a family member. All the things that made every brick of this house stand worthy stood clear before her eyes, all at the same time. All those feelings had mounted into a mourning silence that had developed between the two adults in the past week.

Ben and Susan were inside the car while David carefully locked the main door as if any physical harshness might have had wounded the house. His heart clogged with an unspoken grief too, but he stood with the promise to drown his pain deep within his heart for others around him, and especially his wife. Leaving a home that has kept you well through a crucial phase of your life isn't an easy departure for a man either. However, he was obliged to act practical. Life had taught him that well. So, he held his emotions back, he had a lot to look after.

He quietly locked the door and headed towards the car. The rain continued relentlessly. David adjusted himself on the driver's seat. Martha sat beside him silently aware that there was nothing left to anticipate. She finally stabbed her last wishful hope to a brutal silence. David looked at her once and let his eyes do the rest which words weren't capable of. He ignited the engine and the car took off instantly. Martha turned and stared at the house. A tear dropped from her eye as she whispered her final goodbye, to her home, the one that she would never see again, *ever*.

***

Martha was quiet. While looking outside through the rolled glasses she wondered about their new place. Will it be the perfect house? Will I feel safe there? She addressed these questions worriedly. Above everything, how would Lanthom Cove be? Her mind was choking with tides of unanswered questions.

Raindrops were hitting the car roof callously. It *has never rained like this before*, Martha complained in her mind. The rainwater ran down the windowpanes, blurring the outside view. Ben and Susan were asleep and the sweet rush of their breath was all that contested with the bellow of the thundering clouds. Martha turned at David and was the first one to speak,

"David, are there enough work opportunities in Lanthom Cove?" This was a very valid question and Martha felt stupid for not bringing it up sooner. But she wasn't herself in this past week. She was so involved with her internal dialogue on coping up with this change that she could hardly think about other necessary arrangements. This could have been another valid argument to influence the decision. But then she knew David wasn't stupid. Even if they hadn't discussed this, he would have done his bit. However, she continued, "We would need money to survive. A house can't feed us, right?"

"Yes," David replied calmly despite her challenging tone, "I have enquired about work opportunities in the town. There are some small law firms there that look after all the local cases. I am sure I'll bank a job there. The pay, I am hoping, should be decent enough."

Martha nodded her head slowly on the reply and returned towards the window to gaze outside again. There was nothing else left to challenge; the stamp had been thumped on the verdict.

The green grass flourished along the sides of the roads the car crossed. The dark sky looked duller through the haziness of the frost covered panes. Everything appeared like colours splashed on a sheet of canvas in the name of contemporary art. From beside her, David observed Martha, smiled inwardly, and focused his attention back to driving. There was silence in the car again.

CHAPTER FOUR

"Martha!" she heard a faint voice, "Martha, listen!" she heard it again and it continued, "Wake up!" the voice sounded familiar. "Martha, wake up!!"

She realized it was David.

Martha had slept during the journey. "Open your eyes, honey." She slowly opened her eyes and saw David standing in front of her, smiling with excitement dripping from all over his face.

"What time is it?" Martha asked, yawning. Her head felt heavy caused by the sudden snap out of her sleep. "Why did we stop?"

"It is three in the afternoon and we are finally here! Our new home, Martha, our new house!"

"We have?" Martha said rising eagerly from her seat. She felt an immediate urge to see the house. "Where is it?" An excitement rose in her voice. David pointed with his long-stretched hand and Martha instantly moved her head towards the driver's seat. Her first glimpse of the house was made, and there it was standing right in front of her at a distance from where she could account the whole of it. For a minute she was left frozen. The magnificent view was overwhelming, and it was there waiting for them, the Barcaldine House.

Martha was not anticipating this; it was bigger than she had imagined. She squinted her eyes to get a focussed view.

For a moment, the house even seemed like a rare illusion. But in the next few seconds Martha realized that it was all real.

"Come out, Martha. Come, let's get to it," David shouted moving to the back seats.

"Wake up, Ben! Susan! Wake up, kids. Look at your new house. Come on!"

Ben and Susan woke up due to all the noise. Ben gawked at the house and rubbed his eyes for a clearer view. When he did get a clearer view and widened his eyes in astonishment, David felt a proud joy inside. Then the little Ben asked in his innocent sluggish voice, "Wow, dad, is that our new home?"

"Yes, dear... it is!!" David replied gladly.

Beside him, Susan was equally captivated but kept her reservations. She was not the one to show her feelings right away. But she was silent and her father knew it was a good sign, it meant she was admiring it in her own way. David took both of them out of the car and urged them to head for the house. For a minute, the sadness that came with the change seemed to loosen its grip.

"Martha, come! What are you waiting for?" David called again from a distance. Martha got out of the car slowly keeping her gaze tuned to the house. A faint smile appeared around her lips. It was too windy and her hair ruffled before her face repeatedly. Though it was not raining now, yet the sky was still congested with dense dark clouds making the afternoon appear dusky.

She headed towards the house unhurriedly building a growing closer look. The wind was cold, unusually cold, and her skin got marked with goosebumps. She crossed her hands and rubbed her arms to generate some heat. Within seconds, she was close enough to the house to notice its remarkable details. The mansion stood with a revealing view, erect and unshakable.

First of the many details she observed were the lean lines chiselled on the fine covers of the four pillars. These were the ones holding up the grand protruding porch. The porch had a wide balcony above if someone wished to admire the view of the trees surrounding the house. There were many windows on both the sides of the house, which meant there were many rooms too.

As the family progressed, they could see the three floors, the second and third built like a step above the first one. The middle of the façade reminded Martha of the elaborate Greek carvings she had only seen in big coffee table books. On the ground floor, an open corridor ran under the porch up to the back of the mansion. Ben ran around the whole house in a full circle and found it amusing when he reached the same point from where he started.

Martha was still caught up in the details of the house when the massive gathering of dense trees caught her sight. Together, the mass of the trees was battling with the intense force of the winds. They also shielded the Barcaldine from the back and sides and stood like tall monsters guarding the territory. *Were they guarding someone from leaving the property or getting in?* Such a macabre thought would have left Martha anxious, and it was only good that a possibility so evil never hit her.

A few glades opened and disappeared into the flourishing density of the woods. The depth of the woods could be easily comprehended from the periphery itself. The trees looked mysterious to her; their wild personality did not match the setting of a peaceful old family home. Staring at the trees, Martha murmured, "Creepy"

She retrieved her gaze back at the house. Yes, the same old Barcaldine, but now it was gaining a new tag *The Edments' Residence,* she had already started thinking of a name for the house. Mrs. Martha Edment had already started loving it.

"Martha," David called. He was walking towards her, "So, what do you think, liked it?" he asked eagerly.

"Well......" Martha smiled and looked at him, "I like it"

"Really? Wow! See, I told you you'll love it."

"It's wonderful!" she said admiringly. Martha in her hearty thoughts began to thank lord for not disappointing her. She was contented to know that they owned it.

I will once again settle with my family, it will be a happy home like the one we left behind, Martha thought with a sense of relief.

But who knew it was just the beginning, *beginning of?*

II

The whole family progressed towards the main entrance of the house. Under the porch there were six steps leading to the main central door. David wrapped his arm around his wife and went on like a couple while the kids followed them.

New houses have so much to offer; the smell of fresh paint, shining new polish on the wooden panels, and the pungent smell of stiff rubber outlining the glass frames. But Barcaldine could only offer the sight of old tarnished wood, sharp broken panes, squeaking panels, and various other unsolicited sounds with no hint of their origin. When Martha stepped on the first stair, the wood responded with a little creaking groan. This marked the first human contact of the house in years. None of its dull characteristics could affect or reduce her delightedness. It appeared better than all the new stuff of a shortly built home. But Barcaldine looked different, all such shortcomings were compensated by the grandeur of this old mansion.

However, in the midst of the entire thrill a strange thing happened. Suddenly a cold feeling rushed inside Martha with her first step on the stair. A shudder went through her body seizing her heading feet bringing it to a standstill. In addition to the peculiarity of the experience, it was over within the brush of a second. She stared at David and felt odd because he seemed normal and untouched. Not wanting to disrupt the thrill of the moment, she quickly ignored the strange experience and took the next five steps. Nothing happened. *Maybe it's just the exertion. Maybe it's the air giving me chills*, Martha told herself.

They reached the main door. David took the keys out from the pocket of his faded jeans. He drew a presenting look towards his wife and handed it to her.

"I want you to open the door"

Martha responded with a smile. She took the key that had lost its shimmer probably after decades of rusting inside a hard bottomed safe. She introduced it into the key hole of the double door and turned it. The locks moved with an obliging thud. Martha then pressed on the handle whose surface she found to be icy cold. But the door did not move. She pressed on it again and jerked it a little but it seemed to be jammed. Nothing happened. She tried harder but the door intended not to move at all.

"What happened?" asked David.

"I guess it is stuck. You try it," Martha answered pushing even harder now. She stepped back and David took the position. He grabbed the handle and twisted it. The door moved and unlocked smoothly without showing any resistance.

David grinned at her, "Stuck?"

Martha looked at him in surprise, "That's strange."

"Yeah?" David said teasingly.

"Whatever!" Martha rolled her eyes.

"Well now it is open, let's go in."

He pushed the door. The house was completely dark from inside. One could not see anything through that blinding darkness. It appeared as if the darkness and silence were its only tenants for years, more like one now, blended into one another between these four massive walls. However, the silence was pacifying for some strange reason, even though an old, and unused house ought to be only eerie. But they didn't know that the house had finally retrieved from a deep slumber and the first man-made noise in years was the thud of the locks.

"It is dark," complained Ben.

"Yes, it is. Hold on, I'll switch on the lights and then you all can come inside," David said.

David took out the lighter from his pocket and flamed it on the first hit. He then crossed the main door and was inside now while the others waited for his clearance. It was now visible enough to look for his way. He saw the wooden flooring carpeted with dust that reflected back a hazy image of the thin flame in his hand. Just then, furious lightning surfaced in the sky. The wall on his right flashed for a fraction of a second and there hung the switchboard. He saw it.

"Hurry up, David. The weather is getting worse."

"Yes, I got it."

He rushed for the wall. The flame began to sway under the winds. He reached the wall and hit the first switch he came in contact with. The bulbs flickered and in no time the room filled with gleaming yellow light. Martha hurried inside with the kids. She banged the door behind her and fastened the locks. Finally, they were inside the house. The door handle was still wrapped inside her fist and Martha sighed in relief.

The light shone down brightly from the ceiling of the spacious welcoming space and Martha turned to face the interiors of the Barcaldine. Within a short lapse, the house took everyone's attention. The beauty drenched in the presenting glow seemed irresistible. It began to play its spell sooner than later.

There was no doubt that the interiors did full justice to what they saw outside, equally awe-inspiring, and it managed to keep the excitement going in the Edments. The thundering clouds and the frequent showers were now the worry of the outside world, because around them stood a splendid house, that looked hospitable with its appeasing silence, only that it *wasn't*, but it was too soon to know that.

David joined Martha as he stared all around with eyes wide open.

"This is just so beautiful! I wonder why I never looked inside before." He spoke

"I wonder the same why you never did." replied Martha, her eyes set on the house checking out all the details that were hard to capture at first glance.

"Let's check the whole of it," David said and with this everyone moved to explore different corners.

The house had three floors. In addition to that, there was a basement supporting the house. Martha was delighted to see a good cut drawing room, a well-designed big kitchen, a small room that could be an office or a library, and another comfortable hall that could be considered as a living room. It all reminded her of the gothic setups she thoroughly enjoyed in movies and books.

The ceiling in various rooms stood lavishly tall, drawing a pretentious joy of owning such a lavish property. *Why the hell David never mentioned this house till now?* Martha's internal dialogue went on with things that she couldn't say otherwise.

A wide central staircase took them to the floors above. They found the floor divided into four rooms, one of which was a master bedroom, and a few other private ones. Like the ground floor, the walls even here had a good share of windows for ventilation. Martha could smell the wet cold breeze entering from those rectangular frames. The exit of every room opened into a long common hallway.

Furthermore, the stairs met with the second floor. Some of the notable spaces here were a large balcony at the back, a long study room with racks of books still stacked, and a grand hall. This enclosure was supported by the belt of large windows as seen from outside, also replicated in the master bedroom below.

The topmost floor was particularly a storage place with few smaller rooms designed cheaply and justifiable to be servant quarters. The Edments saw another set of staircases, a rather smaller one, built densely in suffocating passages. It was again connecting all the floors and Martha wondered the use of this extra system. After close observation, she realized that it was also secluded from general access and crossed the denser areas of the house built less luxuriously. It was David who then pointed that it opened closer to the cheaply built rooms and suggested that it might be specifically made for the use of servants. After all, then was an era extreme on class discrimination. In the end, Edments discovered a large attic just beneath the roof.

The wide staircase ended at the crown of the mansion. The top, open to the sky, had a hearty view from where

Martha located a nearby lake and a hill that she missed on accounting during her nap in the car. Everyone explored the place enthusiastically. With each passing minute, they were falling in love with it. The huge rooms, rich wallpapers, expensive flooring, and a classic staircase, all looked well preserved despite the lapse of decades in its care.

A few aberrations occurred, things that could not move on their own or sounds that had no origin. But the Edments were too spelled to notice any such similar deviations that occurred while they strolled around the house. Instead, comparably other trivial matters seemed strangely bizarre to them. For instance, the previous owners had left behind a lot of furniture. From the beds in the two rooms to the furniture pieces in the drawing, a beautiful mirror in the lobby, and a lot more in the basement that included notable possessions like ethnic showpieces, crystal crockery etc. It made no sense why anyone would abandon possessions that held considerable worth. Nevertheless, Martha and David did not bother much. Rather they were too pleased to keep all of it than wonder about someone else's odd decisions.

This was the most unexpected day of their life. The way things shaped up; they never imagined it to be a highly profitable affair. Shifting here now did not seem that bad at all. How quickly perceptions change? It took them an hour more to get introduced to the whole house. By the end of their self-guided tour, everyone had found their adoration for their new house in some or the other way

The hired truck carrying their load finally reached. It was two hours' past since they arrived. Fearing that it might start raining again any minute, the truck driver with the accompanying men unloaded the truck quickly. David made the payments and the truck left back for New York.

It was eight at night and everyone was tired by now. It had been a really long day after all. None of them were left with any stamina or patience to clean the place and make a tidy room to sleep. The best they could do was to change the sheets of the beds well-adjusted in the rooms upstairs. The room was dusty but the choices were limited. The couple obviously opted for the master bedroom and the kids acquired the room just next to them. As no cooking facility was available at the moment, Martha served the family with instant packed food she was carrying. Ben and Susan ate their dinner without any complaints, though for David it was hard to pass the dinner session. He never really relished the packed stuff.

Barcaldine's new inmates suited its personality well and the house immediately sensed it.

CHAPTER FIVE

The couple woke up early in the morning and recognized the call for another hard and a long day. The water facility in the house was working well too, both in the kitchen and in the washrooms. Moreover, as far as the electric connections were concerned, the needful ones were surprisingly fine too. First thing David did in the morning was to fix the coffee machine to help them start their day.

"Isn't this funny? Even though the house hasn't been used in decades and yet it is in a good condition. The water facility, electric connections, everything is working just fine," said Martha. "Seems like well-preserved under the vigilance of a living hand."

Her left palm swayed vertically up and down; just the way it did while making strong arguments in the court rooms during her active years. David noticed the gesture and smiled while he sipped his coffee. "Yeah, it is, and that's a great thing for us. It saves us a lot of money. Otherwise, all that repairing and installations could have cost us big."

Martha nodded in agreement. They sat there for another thirty minutes planning the following days. David decided to give a round in the town in search of men who could fix issues that demanded immediate attention. Martha knew her share of work too. The place was dry and filthy with dust. Their stuff was scattered everywhere on the ground floor. The house was vast and clearly, she could not manage it with just two hands. David was there to provide assistance and so were the kids.

David gulped down the last sip and got up to leave.

"I'll take a shower, got a lot of work to do. You wake up the kids in the meantime."

He kissed Martha on the cheek and went upstairs.

Martha sat there alone for some time. She deeply inhaled the cool morning breeze and drew a glance towards the empty lanes of the hill visible from the window. So many changes had occurred in a few days. She wondered what all they could have had missed if she had denied the offer. But denying was never an option, and that too seemed to make sense now. Something bigger and possibly better awaited them. She didn't want to settle on the idea of better just yet. But bigger, it definitely was! Though the memories of her previous home still lingered close, but Martha was now in a position to consider the future with an open heart. Finally, she felt strong enough, and she realized it was just a matter of time. No doubt, time heals, and it worked in her favour too.

She again noticed the rugged lines of the hill covered with green forests. Few cars ran on its narrow turns and later disappeared somewhere behind. The beauty outside was astounding. Since the night when the demanding decision was made, the weather had become attractively dusky. The day started with a good note.

When Martha went for a shower, David had already left. The cold water running down her body was rejuvenating. She came out wrapped in her bathrobe with water dripping from her hair onto the carpeted floor. Martha quickly dressed herself in comfortable clothes and began to dry her hair while reviewing the master bedroom.

It looked peaceful and composed. The most appealing was its size, almost comparable to an expensive hotel room. *Is it all really true?* she thought as she ran the brush down along the desired length of her hair. Martha studied the furniture already placed in the room. She liked the bed. Some would call it old fashioned, but for her it was vintage, and it suited the interiors well. She decided to keep it. The most exquisite was the cabinet near the set of English windows adorning one of the walls of her room. Its gentle surface seemed vulnerable even to a harmless play of fingers.

Martha left for the next room where Susan and Ben were sound asleep. She peeped through the door and smiled. She stepped inside, walked towards the bed silently, and sat next to her kids. Looking at them, Martha recalled the days of her childhood. The way her parents always loved and protected her, even though she couldn't recognize it then. And now Martha wanted to be the same for her kids. Pulling herself back from the past, she realized it was getting late. She softly ran her hand through Ben's silky hair and whispered,

"Ben, honey, wake up."

Ben slowly opened his eyes and found his mom sitting beside with a glowing face. Martha then softly touched Susan's cheek and she also opened her eyes.

"Good morning, mom," said Susan

"Good morning, honey."

"What time is it?" questioned Susan, yawning.

"It's time to wake up, dear, we've got a long day ahead,"

Martha stepped out of the room and took the stairs leading to the ground floor. Her feet were steady as she got down the stairs. Her one hand slid over the wooden railing behind her. She carried a commanding expression, one of pride, as if introducing her new possession to its master, telling it that she adored it, and in return it had to please her.

As Martha took the last step down, she looked around the hall and turned to her left. It was the way to the basement. She had an eager eye for old things and last night's short trip to the basement registered in her mind. She couldn't go through everything, but realized that whatever was stacked there had an old-world charm to it. She could not wait anymore to explore the treasure locked beneath the house, possibly since ages.

Martha found her way and stopped at the entrance of the basement. She felt eager like a kid who had just received a box full of candies, impatient to rip off the packaging. She twisted the lock and lowered the handle. The door flew backwards and revealed the darkness that was guarding its occupants under shadows. A flight of stairs was leading down and Martha took the assistance of a torch. The yellow light flashed and ripped through the darkness for a safe and clearer way. Her hand reached for the switchboard on the stair passage and she pressed a random button, a right guess that lit up the enclosure. She could now safely get down.

Everything stacked in there was hidden beneath the cover of white sheets that were torn, wrinkled, stained with dirt, and filthy cobwebs. Every item seemed untouched since ages and one could smell the dirt in the air due to zero ventilation. Martha pulled away the covers and more dust flew into the air. She waved the filth away from her face and coughed as she inhaled some of it.

The belongings were antique and beautiful, just as she expected them to be. There were showpieces, old paintings, boxes made of wood with beautiful inscriptions over them, marble carvings, and a lot more.

This looks amazing! Martha thought as she hurriedly reached for the second lot of boxes stacked at the opposite corner.

She was curiously digging through the lot when suddenly something interrupted her and tore away her attention. It was a thud, a loud one. But what was it? Something hit the ground hard. Martha turned to find it out. She looked all around her until she saw it. Something had dropped out from under the covers, out from the stack against the next wall.

She reached for it and lifted it from the floor. It was wrapped in a blue silk piece of cloth, tied with jute rope. She examined it for a few moments, running her hand over the silk that felt soft.

Martha untied the knot and the cloth slipped down. There was a knife. But it wasn't a regular one; it was a large knife, heavy in weight, and finished like an old vintage decorative tool. It was made with great care, that wasn't hard to figure out if one observed its beautiful details. It was definitely not a knife that came to frequent use. It was more artistic in nature than functional. But that did not mean it wasn't sharp. It could have easily pricked the fingers if someone tried to feel its blade to casually check its sharpness.

Martha was intently examining the object when suddenly another sound, a different one this time, interrupted her again. This time it came from the floor above her, somebody was in the living room, and had crossed the hallway in a jiffy.

Must be Ben or Susan looking for me, Martha thought. She hurried leaving everything behind, and headed back. She called for her kids but no one answered. She passed the hallway and stopped at the main door to check outside;

nobody was there either. Martha hurried to the first floor hoping to find her kids in their room. Reaching it, she jerked the door open and stepped inside. Ben was still under the covers, and Susan was nowhere to be seen.

"There you are, still in bed!" started Martha, "And where is your sister?"

The same moment the door of the washroom moved and Susan came out. She seemed to have had stepped out of the bed some minutes ago and clumsily wiped her hands over her nightdress.

"Susan, did you come downstairs looking for me? I was in the basement."

Susan replied getting to her luggage, seemingly uninterested in what her mom was saying.

"No, I haven't left this room since I woke up. Anyway, mom, which one of these bags has my clothes packed?"

"You didn't?"

"Yes, mom, I didn't. Now can you please tell me so that I can go for a shower?"

Susan marched impatiently all around waiting for her stuff to be out. Martha was familiar with Susan's morning tantrums and knew it would be futile getting any answers from her right now.

"Hmm. All right, you go and bathe. In the meantime, I'll get your things out. But just for today. Don't get too comfortable with me getting your stuff ready for you."

"Thanks, mom." She kissed Martha on the cheek and vanished the next moment kicking the door of the washroom behind her.

Martha introduced a nice pair of jeans and a shirt from the luggage and placed it on the bed. She walked out of the room commanding Ben, "Out of the bed, now!" who was still on the pillow trying to get a few more minutes of sleep and sunk himself deeper under the covers at the order.

While exiting, it did strike Martha once again as she murmured, "Who was it then?" She later told herself that it must be nothing but the creaking wood of this old house. It must be the sound of Susan rushing to the washroom. It was too soon to even think that something was wrong, let alone believing that it wasn't the work of a living body.

Later that day, Martha made a to-do list. It was dramatically long with a burden of work that she wasn't equipped to do. It ranged from painting the walls, to cleaning the floors and cobwebs, fixing broken windowpanes, disorientated corners, and what not. In addition to all this, the insane growth of weed all around was blocking the incredible view of the house. It needed a fine cut.

Martha was very particular about order and hygiene. It was hard for her to oversee anything left unattended. When other people chose to hangout and feel pampered over the weekends, Martha prioritized work at home. It was neat of her but David felt she over indulged in it, a reason of their occasional arguments. He was just opposite when it came to this. Nevertheless, marriage is also about adjustments and so they both ruled their way out alternately.

But now, here in this abandoned and deteriorating house, everything demanded attention. Martha was becoming impatient and uneasy with each passing minute. David came home in time. She had just finished making the list and could not wait to show him the burden of work that the house had brought with it.

"Hey, I am back," said David closing the creaky doors behind. Martha was sitting on a couch that was covered with a stained cotton sheet. David walked towards her in his wet boots leaving dirty shoe marks behind. Martha noticed the muck but let it be for now, not wanting to burden her head further.

"Hey, you're back just in time. But how come so early?" Martha asked capping the pen and bundling the sheets of paper in her hand.

"Well, as you already know that l had inquired about a law firm in here. I went to visit them and it turned out they had a vacancy, just what I needed, and," David continued raising his eyebrows and a smile emerged on his face asking her to guess the rest.

"And they hired you?"

"Yes, they hired me!"

He ended it with a flash of a big smile. Martha rose from the couch and hugged him tightly. She was delighted and kissed him to express her joy,

"That's so great, David. l am so happy for us."

The stars were shining upon them; everything was falling right into place. It was the end of another worry. This house was really lucky for them; or was it?

It started to rain hard again, dominating the cries of misery, trying to make them go unheard once again, just when they were needed to be heard, and convey that any good in this house was just an illusion.

CHAPTER SIX

Later in the afternoon when the rains receded, Martha decided to start with minor work first and the next morning she was full on. She started with the ground where the floor was hardly visible, its texture lost somewhere beneath the layers of dirt. Whereas, David took the other issues such as fixing the panes, replacing loose nails, broken wooden planks, and other hundred damages. He hired help that his pocket allowed. Getting the grass done turned out to be the most tedious of all the tasks. Over the years with no care, the garden was full with strong rooted weed, and wild grass that had conquered most of the section of the lawn. Finally, he did manage to clear it after enduring deep cuts that left three days of itch when some of the tiny thorns managed to pass through his flesh.

Susan assisted her mother and Ben his father. Even though Susan was the elder one, she looked younger to Ben. It was largely because of her petite built and height shorter than Ben. But Susan already behaved like a teenager, whereas Ben still was a child.

However, Martha made sure Susan to remember that she was the elder one and she was expected to behave like one. Her mother believed in making one aware of their position in the family. Martha believed in sooner the better. However, at the same time she did not want to hamper the joys of her growing years, thus she maintained a balance.

Ben on the other hand hoped to spend most of the day exploring the house, playing, and doing other activities that the children of his age usually did. But, Martha being Martha, she did manage to find enough work for Ben too, who had no other option but to take it up.

The next week's schedule was strict. The mother-daughter duo started with the drawing room first, reaching every corner, and later headed to the upper floors. The hired help was much needed. The work needed more hands. The three boys from the town, who showed up to earn some extra money, were fortunately laborious. Martha did find them whispering at times, giving Edments looks as if they had a question in mind, or were keeping something unsaid, but she did not care much to know. Fixing the house was a challenging task which occupied the entire day leaving her with no time to worry about a bunch of gossiping boys who might be a little intrigued by the idea of city folks moving to small towns. The demanding schedule lasted for nine days by the end of which the place looked revived.

Finally, the Barcaldine regained some of its shine if not all of it. The air now moved in and around the house more freely, felt clean, and even cold at certain places that Ben constantly complained of as it gave him shivers. The family was settled in the house, and so was the house, with *them*.

CHAPTER SEVEN

The family settled in quite well but it left Martha drained to an extent that she chose to stay indoors for a few more days, relax, and regain her strength before exploring her new surroundings. Even the weather seemed to want for Martha to not leave the house. The skies continuously grumbled and Lanthom Cove bathed under unending spells of rain.

Martha lay stretched on her bed; her head straightened against a pillow. The pages of the book flipped quickly as Martha read an engrossing story. The dusky light and the pacifying silence of the rain helped in setting the atmosphere in her head to perfectly match the plot of the book. Her eyes rushed through the words, unable to tear her attention away. But something did cause an interruption, just when a distracting noise knocked her ears.

It was a faint sound at first but distinguished enough to grab her attention. For a moment she stressed to recognize what it was and stared towards the door as if anticipating to find someone walk into her room any second. When nothing happened in the next few minutes, she got back to reading. She turned the pages when again a similar noise shot out of nowhere. This time it was louder than before, and Martha sat on her bed, alert.

She hurriedly got into her slippers and rushed towards the grand staircase. She gave a lengthy look across the steps in search of signs that could explain the origin of the noise. It sounded as if someone was dragging the furniture downstairs. Martha hurried down the stairs and straightaway barged into the drawing room, only to find all the furniture right in its assigned place. She stood there feeling blank and confused. The glass chandelier swayed lightly above her head.

Suddenly, the same noise was heard the third time, it was even more striking. Martha figured its location; it was coming from the basement. It did not grow any louder but left her frightened. Who wouldn't be after all? Everything unexplained and unknown is still the foundation of all the fears.

Feeling anxious, Martha reached the small door to the basement and pushed it. As she began to descend the stairs, she heard her heartbeat run faster. Within seconds her breathing grew heavy and she discovered why; there was a foul smell reeking from the basement. Martha sensed the uncertainty of the situation and her feet slowed down. Fear found its way into her heart. She wrapped her mouth with her hand to avoid breathing that odour.

As she went down further, a new development flustered her, Martha heard someone crying. The sobs were intense, one coming from a heart trembling in fear. Martha ceased all movements and stood still. She tensed. She pondered to hear closely without making her presence evident. Her ability to decide the next course of action failed her. Martha battled with advancing or staying put as she now grew concerned of her own safety. Will it be safe? Who is it? Who is crying? All such questions started urging and they couldn't be ignored. There was an undeniable need to know, after all everything was happening inside her house. Abiding an impulse, she gathered enough courage to run down the stairs, and find it out herself.

Seconds passed after she had dashed into the chamber of the basement. At first glance, it looked empty. She searched frantically twisting around her shoulders. But then she suddenly spotted it, a clear figure, right in front her. Someone sat against the wall. The figure looked dishevelled with her hands crossed around her knees, and her face buried in it.

Yes, her, it was a girl and above her hidden face, her hair crawled down up to her cramped feet. The sight sent a shot of terror in Martha. She started to sweat nervously and lumps swelled in her throat. In that moment, her mind stopped working, turning numb, unable to guide her any further. Even then, Martha decided to go closer to the girl. She knew it was not the best move, and yet the cries, slowly growing louder and painful, seemed to allure Martha towards her. The girl had sensed Martha's presence. Martha strained to catch a glimpse of her, but the long tangles of hair shrouded her face like a veil.

Is she hurt? Martha thought.

Martha wanted to say something, question, understand what all this was about, but nothing came out of her mouth. The fear consumed her. Even then she felt determined to find out how the girl had made it to her basement.

"Who are you?" Martha spoke with conviction, but her trembling body made her sound shaky. She hesitantly questioned again.

"Who the hell are you?" she was bold this time, "What are you doing in my house!"

To this, the girl grew silent putting an abrupt stop to her cries. It left a deep ghastly silence in the basement. Why was the girl not speaking? Why was there no response? The silence prolonged for several seconds leaving Martha arrested and dominated by fright.

And the girl then lifted her face, and shot an enraged look towards Martha. Martha screamed in horror when she saw that hideous face. She fell back on her feet in shock. The sight was such! That white-blue skin looked pale, and all those bruises made the girl look resurrected from a brutal death. The wounds were fresh and blood oozed from them. Just underneath her chin, a big noticeable slit on her neck testified that she was a victim of a gruesome crime. She kept staring at Martha without a flicker in her eye. Her eyeballs appeared frozen; fixed at Martha's stunned face. Those ferocious eyes finally wavered when tears began to roll out of them, but they weren't expressive human tears, they were tears of blood.

Just then, Martha let out a cry, breaking the knot that had almost choked her throat. The girl was then heard speaking in a dense inhuman voice.

"don't....lhisten...thoo..dehhh..".

The girl struggled hard to finish. She attempted to convey something. But her brutally slit throat could only go that far before she gave up. Her stare shifted from Martha and she looked above her, fixing her eyes at the ceiling. Fear developed in the girl's eyes now. She spotted something there, or was it someone?

The girl began in fear, "No... No..," as if someone was coming closer to attack her. She then let out a cry, like that of a screaming banshee. Martha gathered her shaky feet to run back upstairs. The fear consumed her like the blood running in her veins. She grabbed the staircase, but the panic was too overwhelming, and it made her trip.

She hit her head on the edge of the wooden step. Blood started to run out from her temple but Martha pushed further to stand and take control of her body. She was aware that any more time spent in the basement could lead to something ghastly. But her courage faltered when everything looked dizzy. Martha lost control of herself and instead of claiming her escape, she collapsed and fell unconscious.

One last thought struck her before she slipped into the darkness. My god is with me; she murmured and then surrendered to her fate.

II

She struggled to bring herself back. It felt her body had become stiff as if suffering a fit. Her hands folded into tight fists, her whole body jerked from head to toe, and Martha regained consciousness, only to realize a perplexing reality; she had dreamt a nightmare.

Martha was sweating even in the chilly morning and her body trembled uncontrollably. This sudden retrieve to reality muddled her thoughts. She felt claustrophobic, as if the length and width of her large bed had reduced to a coffin. She threw the quilt away whose heaviness pulled her down. She ran towards the window and pushed it. The panes opened and banged on the exterior walls loudly. Martha could not feel her legs and held tightly to the sill for support. The cool air rushed in and Martha hungrily took a deep breath.

Scenes from the nightmare flashed in her mind again. The effect was still horrifying. The screeching voice echoed in her ears clear as ever. She inhaled frantically, trying to calm down her racing heart. It was only minutes later that the surroundings settled in.

What was that? That was the first question drawn by the shock of the nightmare. Martha wasn't someone who believed in the supernatural. Such unexplained experiences for her were nothing more than fabrications of a fragile mind. Even though the concept intrigued her, she stood by her judgments. But the horrid experience now left Martha to reconsider her own strength. She speculated about the reasons that could lead to her mind concocting such a horrid dream, especially when she knew she was not the vulnerable kind. It was simply disturbing.

Martha was trying to make sense when she heard the click of the doorknob. The door moved half way and David came in holding a hot cup of coffee and a warm smile. Martha shifted her glance towards the digital clock lying on the corner table that read seven-thirty.

"Good morning, honey," David started sweetly while walking towards her. "Here is a nice cup of hot coffee for you, from your favourite person," and added with a naughty expression, "Especially when you plan to start this chilly morning right there at the window in that skimpy nightdress!"

It wasn't the best time for romance. Martha tried to act normal. She greeted him, forced a smile, and continued to look outside.

David noticed her odd reply.

"What happened?" he sounded concerned now, "Are you all right? You look stressed.

"Nothing, I guess it's just a case of bad headache."

Martha at his notice got alert. She did not want to discuss it yet and started rubbing her forehead. She tried to pretend that a headache was the only reason behind her awful morning. David put his arm around her, walked her towards the couch, and made her sit comfortably. Martha bent her head on David's chest.

"Is it really hurting?" he asked. "We can see a doctor if you want?"

Martha knew David would worry the whole day if she did not assure him.

"No, I am fine. I will take a pill. It's just a morning headache; I could not sleep well last night. My head feels heavy now, don't worry," reassured Martha.

"Are you sure?" David stressed again.

"Yeah, I will be alright. You have to leave for work too. If I feel it's not ok, I'll call you," she finally convinced David.

But for how long could she hide it, especially when there were more such instances to come, waiting to snatch her peace away.

CHAPTER EIGHT

It was two in the afternoon and Martha and the kids were done with lunch. Susan stayed locked inside her room upstairs whereas Ben sat on the couch in the living room, unable to decide which channel to stick to. Martha carried the dirty dishes and carefully landed them into the sink. The rush from the tap left sprinkles of water all around the basin. She seldom admitted, but she hated doing kitchen chores. A radio set placed in the kitchen played music from her favourite band and made the work seem bearable. The kitchen was much bigger than the one she was used to working in back in New York. She realized old houses usually had bigger spaces for everything, considering the bulk of hired help that was required to keep everything in order.

After a rough morning, fortunately the day progressed well. Her mother had called earlier and Martha was happy to see her number flashing on the mobile screen. She hadn't been able to speak to her mother lately; there was always something or the other that needed attention. Today she could finally talk. During the call, Martha could not stop praising the house to which her mother followed patiently.

Martha reached for the window and pulled it open allowing the cool breeze in. This was when she saw someone standing outside the main entrance of the house, someone who had been there for a while, but unaccounted.

At first, Martha chose to continue with her work. She bent to get to the lower shelves under the counter. When she got back on her feet; she realized the person hadn't moved at all and was still there. This time Martha grew slightly alert. She gave a closer look and realized it was a woman who had striking red hair. She pretended to do her work while keeping a vigilant eye on the alleged intruder.

When another few minutes passed with no further developments, Martha could not stand it anymore. She threw the wiping cloth on the counter and rushed to the main doors. Reaching there she pulled it open, but it was too late, the intruder was gone!

***

Rains had become an obvious part of the day, an expected seasonal guest that wasn't showing any signs of disappearing anytime soon. The sun had become a rare sight and the showers a constant irritation. It was around evening when it struck Martha to buy some supplies. She got into her slippers, grabbed her purse and umbrella, and was on her way. It was a half an hour affair and made no sense to bother the kids to accompany her in such a weather. And so, Ben and Susan stayed at home after a dull dictation of that old behavioural manual from their mother.

David had taken the car. The second car was sold a few months prior to their move.   She needed the supplies and the grocery store was a few blocks away. She hated getting out in the rain but she told herself that there wasn't an option. The walk till the store went without any hiccups. Martha quickly collected all that she needed in ten minutes, got the billing done, and was on her way back. She clung hard to her umbrella with both hands. The baggage kept slipping out of her grip. Her irritation spiked when she realized some of the muddy water had seeped into her shoes. Just then her umbrella turned along the winds and left Martha completely naked to the rain. It was time to run down the rest of the way. Without any care, Martha shot towards the house juggling with her supplies.

Finally, she slowed down when Barcaldine came into sight, delivering a sigh of relief. The huge tree outside the walls endured the assault of the weather and housed a recognizable body under its old thick branches. But at first, Martha didn't see her, the light was dusky, and the shade of the tree dark like coal. But after a strained look Martha recognized the red hair, done to straight plait. The woman was here again, hiding, when she should be running back to her home somewhere.

What is she doing here? What could she possibly want?! Martha felt provoked this time. She whirled back a wet strand of hair and hastened leaving no chance for her to escape this time.

A pool of water had formed near the curb of the street. Martha's rushing footsteps dashed the water away. Her footsteps could be heard even with the thunder crackling every few seconds and yet the woman did not account Martha approaching her.

At last Martha caught her, grabbed her shoulder from behind, and left the woman startled. The woman turned around alarmed, clear by the shaken look on her face. She gasped and her hand went to her pounding heart. Her breath raced. Seeing her terrified state, Martha took a step back. After giving the woman a brief moment to settle, Martha fired her with questions.

"Who are you? And why do you keep wandering around my house? I saw you this afternoon too!"

The woman began incoherently.

"I'm sorry, I-I didn't mean to scare you."

She finally gulped the anxiety down her throat and introduced herself.

"My name is Amie," she began, "I live nearby, on the lane left to the clock tower," and then continued in her defence, "Please don't think I intend to cause any harm. I apologize for showing around the place in such an odd manner and leaving your worried. But trust me, I didn't mean to cause any damage or as it seemed so," she stressed in an assuring tone.

It sounded genuine to Martha yet she refrained from seeming like someone easy to convince.

"Why do you keep staring at my house?" she questioned promptly.

"Oh!" Amie began and took a sudden pause to measure her answer, "Yes, the house, actually...ummm.... it's just that I have seen this house a wreck all my life, yet always found something very attractive about it. And now with this whole makeover you have given to it, it was quite hard for me to not admire it. I know it might sound weird and merely an excuse for my odd behaviour. But I do apologize again; I seriously didn't mean to frighten you at all."

The woman pressed too hard to prove her innocence. Martha felt finally convinced; it seemed appropriate now to spare her. Besides, she did not actually seem like she could harm anyone. What this petty little creature could have done anyway? With her pouting mouth and bony structure, she looked even more helpless with that anxiety written all over her. Her whole attire and that piece of cloth she was wearing did not compliment her frame at all. The dress made her look lanky. But the red hair was beautiful. Maybe Martha was harsh in her approach, more than she should have.

***

Amie made herself comfortable in the living room. Her hair crumpled into soft curls and water dripped from them trailing the helical twists. She shifted her hair to her left shoulder while looking outside the window and blinking her eyes like an innocent child. Amie rubbed the tips of her fingers against each other and felt her skin go wrinkled due to prolonged exposure to water. For how long had I been standing there? She thought.

The warmth inside the house brought some solace to her shivering skin. A pacifying peace comforted her. She was pleased to be inside Barcaldine and studied the place trying to capture the feel of its ambience. Recalling her sudden encounter with Martha, a faint smile appeared on her lips, thinking about the awkwardness of their meeting, and the realization of her desire now being fulfilled.

Martha appeared heading towards her holding a beautiful tray with two cups placed on it. Amie's head was slightly bent to her right. Her still posture seemed to merge with the placidity of the house. The pair of cups unable to cope up with Martha's steady gait shook. The tinkling of the glass tore the silence and flickered life into Amie. Amie turned her face and fixed an inoffensive gaze at Martha. Both the woman wondered about the nature of their conversation once they were seated face to face. Finally, Martha reached the table. She caressed her skirt from behind and sat on the chair that completed the pair around the table.

"Here, coffee for you," Martha said, "I'm sure you need one."

"Yes, indeed. Thanks a lot,"

Martha smiled

What's next now? The women thought.

Amie sipped the coffee. The warm liquid seeped down all the way through her throat to her abdomen. She had never enjoyed coffee so much as she did it now. It felt like a hard-earned relief.

"So, how long has it been for you since you moved here?" questioned Amie.

"It's been over a month now. Quite a town, I must admit."

"Yes, Lanthom Cove is not big, but it does have its share of surprises, uniquely experienced by everyone."

Martha couldn't comprehend what exactly Amie meant but rather took it as a poetic remark in admiration of the place.

"I wish I could understand what you meant by that," Martha said sounding amused.

"Nothing in particular, it's nothing important. I like putting things in a way that has a hint of mystery to it." Amie smiled confirming her poetic instincts and Martha's good sense of judgment.

The conversation went further during the next hour. Deeper the two strangers dwelled into each other's respective lives, the better they saw their similarities, even if nothing looked familiar about them at the brim. Their meeting was indicating a bridge in formation, connecting the chords of a reliable bond. The earlier impressions were fading already.

Martha learnt that Amie lived with her grandmother who had lived beyond the expected span and was now struggling through the stretch of old age. Her grandmother was the only family left to her history, present, and future at the moment, subjected to her single status at the age of thirty-nine and no motherhood so far.

Amie sat with her legs crossed. She held the cup by its handle and constantly inhaled the soothing aroma of the coffee. Her other hand played with the pearl pendant she wore around her fragile neck. Martha too registered the beauty of her delicate pendant.

"I saw your daughter a few days ago. She was seated in the lawn and going through a book I suppose. She is a beautiful girl," Amie said amicably.

Feeling a sense of pride on the mention, Martha replied with an obliging smile.

"Thank you, her name is Susan, and I'm pretty sure it was a magazine," and she burst out a low-pitched laugh, "You know the generation!"

"Oh, yes. So, who else is there in your family?" questioned Amie.

"Well, I've got a son too; his name is Ben, he is ten, and my husband David. David is a lawyer."

"Sounds like a complete family. Where are the kids right now? Off to school, I guess."

"No school today. They are in their rooms upstairs, probably fighting over something trivial again. Would you like to meet them?"

"Yes of course, I would love to."

Martha nodded and got up. She headed up the staircase. Amie brought her cup closer and took more sips hoping to enjoy her second serve longer before it got cold. Ten minutes had passed when Martha reappeared.

Susan was the first one to step forward and address Amie. Her mother never interacted with people that easily. It was strange to see how her mother had invited this woman inside their home. To Susan, Amie looked like someone who had been abandoned by the world and needed help. What seemed even weirder was that her mother wanted them to meet her. It was all a very new situation to Susan whereas Ben was too young to even cite the difference."

Martha introduced her kids and Amie responded, in Martha's view, with warmth. Contrary to what her mother noticed; Susan found Amie awkward. She found her distracted and cold towards them. Amie seemed engulfed in her thoughts as if she were calculating something. When greeted by Susan, Amie replied in a scattered tone as if even that little effort bothered her. The young girl tried to put a few more words to carry the conversation. Amie replied to Susan but bridged nothing further from her end.

"I think it's late now," Amie said getting up from the chair. "I should be hurrying otherwise I'll miss out on a lot of work. Thanks for the great coffee, Martha. I'll see you around."

"It was a pleasure for all of us too. Let me walk you till the gate."

"Goodbye, Susan. Goodbye, Ben, I am really glad to meet you all," the words rushed and Amie left.

Ya right! Thought Susan, nevertheless she forced a smile.

CHAPTER NINE

Amie fled the way back to her home. Her clothes were still damp and stuck to her body, leaving marks on her soft skin beneath. The Barcaldine's interior was cozy and comfortable, and back in the cold, her body began to lose its warmth again. She crossed her arms, locking them tightly, and quickened her steps.

Amie gritted her teeth, failing to distract her thoughts, not from feeling an unbearable chill, but from what happened inside Barcaldine during those minutes when Martha left to fetch her kids. It wasn't an imaginary passing blur that appeared before her eyes. However, she wanted to believe so because otherwise it meant that her mind was playing tricks with her again, and if that was true, she had every reason to worry.

Ironically, she would have felt much assured if it was a ghost, trapped inside Barcaldine, turning active again. But her past was refusing to let that affirmation sink in, and suddenly Amie found herself recalling a long-forgotten phase of her life that she swore never to remember. She promised herself never to recount those difficult chapters of her youth, allowing them to resurface. But what happened today flashed all the memories before her eyes vividly. Is it possible? Is it all coming back? A tornado began to circle in her head, questioning her repeatedly with hopes of receiving some suitable answers.

She collectively remembered the beginning of the twenty-third year of her life when for the first time she saw that apparition or as later cited by her psychologist; figment of her imagination. It all started one night after her return from a colleague's birthday celebrations, just two days after her own.

Exhausted after the night, she unstrapped the ties of her glamorous dress that hung on her shoulders and released it in one go. The dress fell on the carpeted floor. After pushing the dress aside with her foot, she walked to her mirror table and sat on the settee. Fluffing a piece of cotton and plunging it into the toner, she started to wipe off the layers of makeup applied to accent her features already at peak beauty. She stared at her delicate pearl piece, gifted by her grandfather, in awe of its beauty and how well it suited many of her attires. It was perfect and she adored it as a valued family treasure, a reminder of her loved ones being near and close. It had the same shine as that of her youth.

Amie looked at her delicate hands and its long fingers adorned with fine rings inherited from her dead mother. How beautifully the colourful gems highlighted her fair skin. Those beautiful hands reached for her head, where a dazzling hair piece clipped her soft curls, revealing a thin and slightly long but desirable neck. She gently took out the clip and those heavy tangles fell on her petite shoulders. She loved being young and beautiful, and nonetheless, desirable.

Her curls looked dazzling but she always made a point to straighten them before going to bed. Amie reached for the hairbrush but hit its handle before she could grab it. The brush fell under the mirror table. She knelt down to restore it. Once she grabbed it, she swiftly straightened to face the mirror again, and then suddenly, everything changed. A reflection was visible in the mirror, alongside hers. Amie felt a short cry inside, but only silence followed the shock. It seemed as if her throat had been locked. She couldn't scream or call for help. She was detained to focus and then the figure became clearer. It was a woman, her attire looked old-fashioned, standing right behind Amie against the wall. It looked hazy but clear enough to capture its details. Amie quickly turned to see who it was but the apparition had already vanished. It faded with such quickness that she couldn't even track its disappearance or register the validity of the whole event. Amie lived an indelible nightmare that night.

For the first few hours, she tried to assure her mind that it was nothing, or probably something caused by exertion. After all, she had had a couple of days of incessant activity. She tried hard to talk her mind into it. Whatever it was, it was vivid and detailed, and if this wasn't a byproduct of her exerted mind, she had every reason to worry. She did not believe in ghosts, nor in God. An atheist she was. However, she knew such disorders could not surface overnight and she wasn't facing any downfalls that could interfere with the functioning of her well-being. But there was another possibility that she didn't want to consider. The disease had engulfed her mother. The symptoms were diagnosed in her grandfather too. They said mental health concerns were hereditary. Was it her turn now?   And with this realization, the real damage struck. Amie successfully talked her brain into believing that unknowingly somewhere beneath the depths of her mind, a disease was breeding, and tonight it managed to take over, the same disease, the same darkness that ran in her family. She was the new victim.

Days passed and with that the visions increased. They progressed from being hazy and occasional to clear and regular. She believed that her acknowledgement of the illness had only worsened her situation, and she was unable to reverse the effect. In the end, she cursed herself for thinking that she was untouchable, that she had full control over her mind, and that nothing could ever hinder her sense of stability, whereas she should have been more careful considering the history of her family.

But the damage was done. The impact of that night followed by guilt and blame weakened her to an irreversible extent. The mental downfall marked a struggle of three years during which she felt frequently exposed to destructive thoughts followed by numerous attempts to fight her visions, and countless sittings with the psychiatrist. The disease hindered the flow of her life abruptly. With every setting sun, she only feared what new complications could emerge and materialize before her only to stay with her in the following days. Her life turned hollow with no job, zero relationships, and minimal friends. Amie suffered a dent that changed her, and made her into someone who had no resemblance anymore to the person she once was.

No amount of love could hold back the sanity she could feel slipping away. The second year of struggle became worse when the hallucinations turned palpable. Sometimes the woman sat against the wall cross-legged and at times followed her to the bed and lay down beside her. It would then caress Amie's neck and roll Amie's pendant between her fingers. Amie hated that. As per the psychiatrist, Amie feared that this imaginary companion would steal her pearl pendant, something that was close to her, and the remaining fragment of the person she once was. This indicated another human insecurity. How one's mind could play with them? Mind or Brain? It did not make any difference. It hardly mattered to Amie; philosophy had no space in her life.

Insomnia had declared its stay. She would spend hours sitting at the window during starry sleepless nights and follow the phases of the moon. During those dark hours, the visions would re-appear only to provide its discreet company.

She considered suicide on various occasions. However, if not her mind but her heart was still receptive of her grandmother's love and concern visible in those sunken spectacled eyes. This fortunately restrained her from choosing the dark road to death. She also remembered what psychics said about the afterlife of the victims of suicide, but it was the secondary reason. For Amie, living a dark isolated afterlife seemed easier than to continue with this hideous creature attached to her identity like a shadow. The only option left to her was to play numb. But how could one possibly turn ignorant to such a self-created misery? Especially when it followed you everywhere like a shadow. Amie may shroud her face or blink her eyes several times to push the visions away, but only a stubborn refusal followed. The disease had penetrated her core by then.

Amie shivered and pulled the strings of her memory back to the present; the remembrance had become almost vivid. She grabbed the doorknob of the entrance to her house and realized that her palms had gone wet with cold sweat. The memory was equally horrifying as the experience years ago. Amie sensed a strange numbness towards the world around her. The objects familiar to her acted powerless in pulling her back from the recollection of an unforgettable past. Forcefully, she tried to concentrate on the objects around her; the flower pot resting beside the couch, the candle stand acquiring the center of the table, the books that had helped her, her parent's photo, but nothing had the intensity to remind her of the person who ages ago had moved on from that immortal past.

Amie checked her grandmother's room to see if she was resting like usual. She always peeped inside her grandmother's room after returning home and so she did today only to assure her grandmother that everything was mundane and normal. Avoiding any unscheduled noises, she headed towards her room, locked it and threw herself on the bed.

The tension in her mind was still persistent. Why am I pondering on it? Is it necessary to relate it to my past? These were the first series of thoughts that came forward to defend her failing stability. Maybe it wasn't a good idea to indulge in such a recollection. She quickly went through the defence mechanism her psychologist had taught her during the initial stages of her recovery; the process of counter questioning, weakening the negative plot of the mind with questions that could weaken the durability of a false idea.

So, Amie began to chant a series of defensive thoughts. "It is not the truth. It is irrational and has no foundation to it." A reasonable victory was felt; self-assurance was working. At the same time, she could notice the striking similarity between this moment and the night that changed the identity of a much sociable and exuberant Amie. Now she had come a decade forward. Fearing the fatal symptoms to find a host again in her head, Amie refused to indulge any further in the war of thoughts, covered her head with cushions, and forcibly slept.

CHAPTER TEN

The next morning Martha discovered an envelope lying on her table addressed to The Edments. It was a dinner invitation from David's colleague Mr. Richard Dylan on the occasion of his wedding anniversary. To Martha's delight, it was a perfect opportunity to step into the crowd of Lanthom Cove and find her footing. After all, even Susan and Ben needed to widen their circle in the neighbourhood.

As Lanthom Cove was a small town, the Dylans lived only a few blocks away across their street and were expected to invite other affluent families. Martha later learnt that Richard was at a much higher post than David's. He was also a very wealthy man blessed with the capacity to afford any luxury to suit his comfort. Law was his passion, so money was not the driving force. Mr. Dylan had various family establishments to sustain his wealth. David was one of his newly found favourites and Richard was enthusiastic about introducing him to his inner circle. It seemed like an on-time opportunity to Martha. Her house was ready to receive guests, she had got accustomed to the place, and the rest of the voids were to fill once she made some potential acquaintances. She recalled meeting Amie. She had developed a liking for the woman and was also looking forward to see her again.

Martha's pick for the night was a knee-length black dress, a supple stole to wrap around the narrowness of her shoulders, a pair of diamond danglers to dazzle her ears, and support of light makeup to make sure it had just the right effect. The best feature of her face were her voluptuous lips that she made even fuller by applying a random tip that always worked for her.

· The invitation was for seven in the evening and the venue was Dylan's residence. David made sure to reach the venue on time and seem well mannered to his host. He could spot the venue from the approaching distance; sparkling under the spell spun by bright and beautiful lights. It already promised an unforgettable evening. The inside of the manor was equally compelling; the contemporary style suited the interiors. When the Edments entered, Martha couldn't miss noticing the couches and drapes, which all in her opinion, without a doubt, were exported from the best of the places. Edments had only made it across the entrance when they saw the Dylans heading towards them. Richard led the way with his wife a few steps behind him. He enthusiastically waved towards David and steadied his steps.

"Welcome, David, we are glad you could make it."

"Thank you, Mr. Dylan. We had to come; without a doubt." David replied with a flush of smile. He was obliged to appear equally thrilled especially after scoring enough personal attention from a senior.

"Very well, David." A few more laughs followed and then Richard addressed Martha, "So, who is this beautiful lady accompanying you?"

David hurriedly turned towards Martha and introduced her, "This is my wife, Martha, and our kids, Ben and Susan."

"Hello, Martha, it's a delight to meet you all. How are you, kids? I hope all is going well with the new place."

Martha greeted him with a gracious nod and a beautiful smile.

Mrs. Dylan finally appeared after facing much delay when she spotted some minor errors while crossing the dinner table and managed to get them rectified before her attention flickered to comparatively other bigger flaws. This undoubtedly was Mrs. Charlotte Dylan, a control freak, famous for throwing the best dinners around the town, only to flaunt her wealth and exquisite taste. She was not exactly an arrogant woman. She was at least, due to her clean upbringing, quite civilized to the people she dealt with personally and professionally.

"Ah! Charlotte," Richard stretched his right arm towards his wife and received her. Charlotte firmly stopped into the periphery of his long arm that Richard immediately wrapped around her bony shoulders.

"Meet my wife Charlotte, and, Charlotte; they are the Edments I told you about."

"Hello, Mrs. Dylan, we are pleased to meet you," started David and added remembering the occasion, "Congratulations on your anniversary, to both of you. I am sorry I didn't wish you earlier, Mr. Dylan. I wanted to wish the couple together."

"It's ok, David. And please call me Richard. Mr. Dylan is too formal."

"Certainly, Mr. Dylan – I mean, Richard." A hesitant smile marked his lips. To Martha, it was obvious that David did not expect such a level of hospitality at this stage of interaction.

"Thank you for your wishes. We are pleased to have you here," replied Charlotte with a tone articulated to suit a woman of her status.

"Charlotte, this is my wife, Martha."

"Our wishes to both of you. You have got a beautiful place around here, Charlotte, very appealing," Martha said.

"Thank you, Martha; I have put in a lot of work on the interiors." This time Charlotte was more enthusiastic in her reply and this instantly made Martha more agreeable and likable as a person to Charlote.

"I am sure we don't plan to spend the whole night over here; rush in everyone and join the guests!" Richard directed the Edments with his usual candid tone.

"Yes, please join the crowd," said Charlotte after her husband.

The couple seemed a little odd for each other, a cheerful man with a little too stiff a woman beside him.

Edments got a chance to meet various people residing throughout the calculable expanse of Lanthom Cove. David met a few others from his workplace. Not much time had passed since they arrived, but Martha could already spot the appreciation in the eyes of men for her and the growing insecurity in women, a clear indication that she indeed had made an impression. A gathering that was tagged as small still housed around seventy people, which was quite long for a cozy guest list, but not for the house hosting it.

The rhythm of the night was gearing up. Glasses of wine and champagne were pouring in. A flock of waiters distributed around the hall with the starters. The Dylans had made special arrangements for the children on the first floor of the residency who were accompanying their parents. They had their own kids too and made sure to keep the ground floor restricted only to adults.

About a half an hour later, holding a sleek crystal glass of champagne, Martha stood below the chandelier in conversation with a few other women. She talked about the place and her experience back then as a lawyer in New

York. That night Martha encountered many people with interesting work profiles. One was an architect working with an established firm in New York, a close acquaintance of Dylans, and had specially travelled over the weekend to join them. A woman, a senior in handling the workings of the national museum of Lanthom Cove, an archaeologist by qualifications, had joined too and introduced a very unique tangent to the conversations that were being carried out. David also seemed occupied with his colleagues and their extended connections. The interiors were warm enough, kept so by the embers of burning wood in the beautiful chimney designed at one end of the hall and could easily have been one of the biggest chimneys Martha had ever seen.

After her brief conversations, Martha strolled around the hall with her glass still wrapped inside her long fingers. It was her third serve of the wine. She was thoroughly enjoying being at the Dylans and definitely needed this, especially after the rush filled weeks that were now behind her. She was further exploring the house when at a far corner of the lobby she saw a group of men and women, around eleven in number, who stood distributed around a single couch, completely engrossed in the words of a man who must have been in his late sixties.

The man seemed to have had hypnotized his audience with his passionate speech, which Martha could make out by the fluctuating tension in his expressions. He was probably narrating an interesting incident, but his words were not audible from where she stood. Charlotte approached Martha after she spotted her standing all alone at a corner.

"Enjoying yourself, dear?"

"Charlotte!" Martha did not notice her approaching. "Oh yes, of course, everything is exquisite."

"I am glad to hear that."

Both the women smiled on their remarks.

"That is Edward Woods," Charlotte said slightly pointing her finger towards the man on the couch. She had noticed Martha staring curiously at the group.

"He is a rare figure to be seen in public. Actually, his profession makes him so," muttered Charlotte under her breath.

Martha slightly bent her neck to listen to her closely. The statement evoked interest in her.

"Really, what does he do?" Martha questioned keeping her eyes fixed on the man.

"He is a paranormal researcher, in fact one who is quite well-known with an experience of almost three decades behind him. He is considered quite a marvel in his field."

This readily took Martha's full attention.

"Wow! A paranormal researcher! That's a very engrossing subject."

"You seem to have an interest for it."

"Yes, I do. The unexplained has always intrigued me," replied Martha, the excitement still persistent in her eyes.

"Well, then, why don't you join the group? You would get to hear some incredible stories. Come with me."

"Sure."

Martha and Charlotte on reaching the group and without creating any disturbance quietly got seated on the couch next to Mr. Woods. There was one more listener already sitting on it.

Mr. Woods continued his passionate speech.

"The world of paranormal, to most people, is like air. It is all around you and even though it is not apparent to the naked eye, yet it can be felt. Occasionally we do get connected to it, and often it is felt as a gut, intuition or the presence of an unknown something around you. But its factuality is usually dismissed due to lack of concrete proofs that can be easily understood by our five senses. However, that does not mean this other world doesn't exist. It is as real as you and me, and only our perception of it marks its validity in our lives. Throughout my study of the subject so far, I have understood this world to hold its own mystical reality, which is tangible to only those who are more prone to the unseen or are ready for it. This invisible world circulates with an energy that adheres more to the subconscious mind rather than the conscious one."

Now Martha knew why the listeners appeared to be hypnotized, the words had their own mesmerizing grip. Mr. Woods was resting against the back of the couch. His legs were crossed over each other and reflected on his composure and hold over the crowd. While he spoke, he didn't look at his audience directly, but stared somewhere at a distant point, completely captured by his recollections. Every member in the crowd had their drinks in hand, but they forgot to sip from them. His words had their own high.

"In the past two decades, I have met various people with capabilities which you and I might not have. With them, I have worked in depth, along with the assistance of science, on various unexplained occurrences. You would be surprised but we have been able to capture images of energies commonly quoted as spirits and ghosts, and also tape their voices and messages they are desperately trying to convey, a phenomenon that in our field is termed as EVP-Electronic Voice Phenomena."

"How is that possible though? I mean if there is nothing to see or hear, how can these devices then capture them," someone asked from the crowd.

"Excellent question. The reason that spirit impressions can be taped or captured on a photographic plate is because they resonate on a different energy spectrum, unlike that of our physical world. And because of this difference, these impressions are not perceptible to our senses. But they are vulnerable to these devices. Animals too can tap into this energy zone, which is why they can know and identify a foreign presence easily and react to them. For a dog, certain colours have no meaning, but that doesn't mean the world is grey, the dog merely lacks the perceptibility, and likewise we humans for the supernatural."

Hearing this, the crowed looked convinced. For their set of beliefs, it was hard to understand, even though they wanted to.

"Mr. Woods, you said that the two worlds co-exist simultaneously, so is it possible that these worlds can also get mixed up at times?" another question came from the audience.

For the first time Mr. Woods turned his face towards the people patiently playing the role of a discreet audience. The question pulled him back to the world around him. There was surprise in his eyes. He began to answer but was suddenly at loss of words? Could it be that his experience defied him for a flicker of a moment? But in the end, despite of whatever reservations he had, Edward continued.

"The moment when it happens, when the two worlds get caught up in the same web of existence, and if one refuses to accommodate the other, something unforeseen always happens. Nothing good can come out of it. No matter who wins, it is always at the cost of some loss," said Edward.

For the first time the man let fear surface in his eyes. To make it go unnoticed, he closed his eyes towards the end of his answer. The audience failed to interpret the message, but fear managed to creep into their hearts too. Martha didn't realize; but she was sincerely following the conversation. The wine had its effect and so the words registered with ease and intensity. She was the only person in the group with no reaction, neither had she seemed to agree or disagree. Her mind was obscured. Mr. Woods opened his eyes, took a deep breath, and turned his head towards the guests.

"I hope that explains everything," he said twitching his lips into a deliberate smile.

He noticed Charlotte and the woman accompanying her. He nodded towards Martha acknowledging her joining the audience.

"You definitely know how to scare the hell out of us, Edward," Charlotte began and followed it with an awkward laugh. She registered the tension in the crowd and herself felt goosebumps. It was time to lighten things up.

"One must never miss a chance!" Edward winked at her. and laughed heartily. Only moments ago, he looked like a man with no affinity towards the normal world, but now turned more congenial to his surroundings.

***

As the night advanced, the dinner was set with a variety of selected cuisines. Charlotte for the evening listed the menu herself. According to her, agreeing with the caterer's selection for the menu was equivalent to inviting a failure for dinners. Charlotte wasn't letting that happen. Not at her dinner party. Hence, her intervention was not only prudent but imperative.

The aroma of the food was rich. The guests had already begun appreciating everything and Charlotte was pleased with the final display of the night. Martha started with some Mexican specialties. She had only begun serving her plate when she heard a voice from someone standing next to her.

"Hello, we haven't been introduced yet."

Martha turned and found Edward Woods, still with his glass of wine, and the newly acquired congenial mood.

"Hello, Mr. Woods," Martha shifted the plate in her left hand and shook hands with him. "I am Martha Edment."

"Hello, Martha, it's a pleasure to meet you. I hope I didn't scare you with my speech earlier."

"No, not all. In fact, it was quite thrilling to hear about your experiences. Mrs. Dylan told me about you. It is not often that we get to meet someone like you."

Edward had met various people who appreciated his work, however not genuinely, but only to not seem rude otherwise. And by now Edward had learnt to differentiate quite well. Even though his work was much acclaimed, yet for many, it was absurd, and a clever depiction of superstition to fool the innocent, only to breed fame out of it. That had always been the challenge for people who dealt with paranormal for a living and it was no different for Edward. However, Martha appeared genuinely interested which could be seen in her enthusiasm. The same genuineness was also evident in her silent amazement back with the group and which also motivated Edward to come and personally meet her.

"Oh, that's very kind of you, Martha. I am always eager to share my research with people."

Edward asked the passing waiter to refill his glass while he continued.

"I have attended many dinners hosted by the Dylans, but I have never seen you before."

"Yes, that's true; we have recently moved to Lanthom Cove."

"Okay, that certainly explains it," Edward smiled and sipped from his glass of wine.

"My husband, David and Mr. Dylan, work for the same firm. He is a lawyer too," Martha pointed towards David who busily carried discussions with a few of his colleagues.

"Your husband looks like a fine man," Edward remarked.

Martha smiled.

"So, how do you find Lanthom Cove?" Edward continued.

A waiter interrupted and offered Martha champagne. Martha picked a delicate glass filled with golden coloured drink and drew a thoughtful glance before she replied.

"It's a nice congenial town. Though very different to where we come from in New York, everybody seems to know everyone in here." Martha laughed quietly and then added, "But it's certainly comfortable. Initial days were a little difficult with all the renovations; ours is quite an old house, but we are very much settled now."

"Really, which house? As far as I know there are hardly any old buildings left in here?"

"I don't know if you have heard the name, it's just a very old house," Martha tried to be modest.

"Try me."

"Okay. Well people recognize it as Barcaldine House, though we have now changed it to just, The Edments."

Mr. Woods was sipping his wine but suddenly froze. The rim of the glass was still in his mouth while he stared at her with his bulging eyes. He then quickly lowered the glass, gulped the wine forcefully, and cleared his throat to speak.

"Oh! Barcaldine, yes – mmm - heard of it. Tha- that place was vacant for decades, so maybe it slipped my mind," Richard began to stare towards the floor as he spoke. He stammered and his tone became dry and hurried.

Martha noticed the sudden awkwardness.

"Mr. Woods, is everything alright?"

"Yes -Yes, dear. I am fine," Edward chuckled nervously.

He looked around the crowed, engrossed in their hopeless conversations on mundane issues. Certainly, an unexpected weirdness trimmed his easy self.

"You bought the house recently?" inquired Edward.

"No, my husband has owned it for quite a long time now. He basically inherited it."

"Have you or your husband been here before?"

The tone of his questions was very straight now as if he was interrogating. Martha could understand that he was stressing to conclude something. Every passing second made her only more uneasy.

"No, this is our first time. I wasn't even aware about the property till we decided to move."

To her reply, Edward inhaled deeply raising his chest. He crafted his next question abruptly.

"Are you aware...," he gave a few more moments to decide whether to push further or not, but then he did, ".... of its history?"

"What history?" Martha said.

It was more of an expression than a question from her. The noises in the hall seemed to go faint and Martha had her eyes fixed on Edward.

Edward sensed the alarm. I shouldn't have mentioned it, he thought to himself. He studied her expressions quickly and realized that Martha clearly did not know what he was getting at. *This isn't the best time to talk about it.*

He suddenly burst into a laugh, a deliberate fake laugh. The immediate need was to lighten up the conversation quickly.

"What happened, Mr. Woods?"

"Look at you; did I manage to freak you out this time?"

Martha felt embarrassed and quietly chuckled when she realized the situation. *So, he was one of those witty ones.* How people can be so unpredictable, Martha wondered.

That was close, Edward anxiously concluded. This woman was not someone gullible who could easily be pushed into believing things. She certainly did not buy his lie, at least not one hundred percent. However, she couldn't have comprehended easily that there was something terribly wrong about his recent remark even if he was lying now. He sipped the champagne that tasted a bit bitter now.

"Anyway, Martha, you enjoy your food before it gets cold. It was nice meeting a charming woman like you," Edward said on a closing note.

"And it was the same for me, Mr. Woods."

"Very well..."

They shook hands and Edward turned to get lost in the glitter of the night. For a few seconds, Martha stood there looking at him walk away. The food in her plate had gone cold but retained its rich taste. She gulped a few more sips of the champagne and went on to serve herself dinner.

Edward, even while talking with the others later, could not detach his mind from thinking about the Barcaldine and their new inmates. Haven't they felt anything yet? Are they even aware of what happened inside that house? Such questions battled in his mind and the June of 1976 kept bouncing back to his memory. He precisely remembered that unfortunate night after which he never dared to step inside that house again or return to investigate it even after he became a paranormal researcher, especially when he could have. He even dreaded hearing about it and talking of its past was strictly unthinkable. Yet, he considered reaching out to her. Should I see her in person and tell her the truth? Edward questioned to himself.

He felt an immediate urge to disclose the events to the new owners of the house, but he knew that it was neither the best occasion nor the suitable place to discuss something so dreadful. But somehow, he had to find a way to reach them later. After all, it was their home now, the place where they wanted to feel safe, even when Barcaldine was far from comforting and which, in his opinion, was a doorway to hell.

***

That whole night Edward couldn't sleep. He lay restless on his pillow and was unable to cease the collision of thoughts blocking his head. He had to speak to Martha. By now, he was sure that none of the Edments were aware of that tragedy.

"I have to... I just have to..."

CHAPTER ELEVEN

The next morning arrived with the usual of Lanthom Cove. The predictable rain marked the beginning of another sluggish day. Ben and Susan complained about the rain, hoping to get a day off. But much to their disappointment, they were sent off to school by the scheduled time. David as per his routine was now sitting in his cabin juggling through some fresh civil-case files.

Martha on the other hand was at home, on her couch. There was a time when she wouldn't know what to do with time off from work. She would get anxious at home not knowing how to busy her fidgety mind that only found peace and meaning in spotting loop holes in the narratives of the opposition party. But now, after years of detachment from the busy life of a lawyer, she had learnt to enjoy life outside of courtrooms. And her most recent victory was the transition from New York to Lanthom Cove, a difficult one though, but she managed to pull through it quite well. This afternoon to herself was indeed welcoming.

She picked up the book resting on the side table, the table that David now liked to call as the branded one. Martha once mistakenly forgot to use a coaster, and the hot mug burnt a round crusty impression on the wood. David now liked to tease her with his remark, and it always made her reply with a 'I hate you!' But in truth, she liked to be teased by him. It had its own rhythm of love and laughter.

And just like that, it left a smile on Martha. She placed a coaster before resting the mug she had brought from the kitchen and went on reading.

The book spoke about a man fighting for his dreams. After reading for an hour, she kept the book down, and looked outside the window. The passionate descriptions in the book made Martha turn pensive. The rage of the rains had made the view from the glass blurry. Only a faint suggestion of the trees standing rigidly upright was visible.

Martha picked the coffee mug, brought it near her lips, and realized it was empty. She lifted the book, inserted a bookmark, and began towards the kitchen to refill her mug. She pulled up her slipping pyjama and then the sleeves of her oversized sweater. In this casual attire, she looked more like a girl in her early twenties rather than a woman in her late thirties.

The inside of the house had gone dark. The light reaching from the sun subdued by dark clouds wasn't enough. The floor beneath her feet felt unusually cold even though the heater was on since morning. However, the coffee was still warm in the kettle that saved her the labor of reheating it.

The clouds thundered again and Martha grumbled at the shrivelling sound of it. It could wake up the dead, it was that loud, and Martha hated how it made her jump on her feet. It had been the same since morning. The wind had grown stronger all around the house and she could hear the twittering sound of wooden branches hitting the roof.

Martha was heading back for the living room when she heard the light flickering. The lamp hanging in the hallway dimmed and then grew bright abruptly. It was heading towards a fuse. She jumped towards the switchboard to avoid the bulb from burning out. But before she could make it, a low blast occurred and all the lights in the house went off. A slight smoke emerged from the lamp and Martha understood what had happened. Not only the bulb but something in the household electrical system had burnt out too.

The hallway looked more like a dungeon now and only the faint grey light from the sky was her support. There was still time for David to return and with Martha's little knowledge about the electrical matters; she knew she had to do without it for the whole day. She remembered putting a bunch of candles in the cabinet stationed near the staircase. Nothing was visible in the kitchen but still she managed to locate a box of matchsticks.

She pulled the matchstick out and bruised the tip against its small cardboard box. The stick ignited with a fuming flame and she began to light the wick of the candles, just when there was a knock on the main door. She let out a complaining gasp, extinguished the stick, and turned to answer the door. She opened it to receive the unusual guest.

There was a man of about her age, almost six feet tall, and his clothes looked like a uniform, something that wasn't in custom anymore. On his right stood an umbrella the black fabric of which was detained with fresh rain.

"Good afternoon, madam," he started, "sorry to knock on your door like that, but I guess the doorbell isn't working."

He appeared well mannered and adequately courteous.

"Good afternoon," replied Martha. She couldn't recall when was the last time someone called her madam and that too with an English accent.

"Yes, a fuse occurred a few minutes back." She paused for a moment and then said, "How may I help you?"

"Certainly, Madam. My name is Henry Beckett. I have been sent by Mr. Edward Woods to deliver you this."

From his tuxedo jacket, he produced a white envelope and offered her to take it.

Martha took a few seconds to recognize the name. *The man at the Dylans!*

She took the envelope from him and questioned while examining it.

"What is it?"

"I have no idea, madam. But I have been asked or rather ordered – as I must mention – to wait for your response after you see it."

His tone was straight and formal, clearly abiding the instructions.

Martha eyed him in confusion.

"I would be right there, near that car, with my umbrella of course," he pointed towards a shining black Benz, "Do let me know whenever you are done, Madam," he finished speaking and waited for Martha to reply.

But Martha did not know how to respond to this odd conversation. First, she needed to understand why all of a sudden this man was visiting her? What was in this envelope now in her care? And what exactly wait-for-a-reply meant?

She anticipated further explanation and when it didn't come, she merely replied with, "Umm ...okay," which indeed sounded like, *I don't understand the hell you are talking!*

"Well, then, good afternoon." He lowered his hat and turned pushing out his umbrella.

Martha looked at the envelope and then at the chauffer heading towards the car. She lifted the fold and inserted her fingers into the envelope. A wrapped sheet of paper came out sticking beneath the grip of her fingers. She unfolded it and there were words, hand written, and she began to read them curiously.

Martha,

After a tough debate with myself and a lot of thinking, I realized I would greatly regret on personal grounds and also as a paranormal researcher, if I do not write this letter to you. It might seem odd of me to approach you in such a manner, but it was important that you decide on your own, and not under any pressure, as to what you must do with the information I am about to share with you.

Last night, during our conversation, you noticed a slight change in me when you spoke about your house. To which, let me clarify now, that you are a sharp observer – you were right! It did startle me, out of fear, when you said the name that no one has mentioned to me in the last, and almost, 29 years now, and it brings shivers in my body even now when I talk about it here.

Now let me get straight to it.

The remark that I slipped off as a joke during our conversation was in fact true; Barcaldine does have a history, and I know that neither you nor your family is aware of it. It is something that must be told to you, before anything fatal occurs...

It is my request that you meet me at my residency, which is in Lanthom Cove itself, as soon as possible. My Chauffer will escort you at your suitable schedule. Do mention the time and day when I should expect you and when Henry must pick you from your home. If you need time to think more, please take it, and then decide.

You would find one more slip inside the envelope that has my address and phone number mentioned on it, in case you do not wish to reply right away.

However, I would suggest; make haste and accept my invitation.

Please don't ignore this.
Edward Woods

"What is this?" Martha muttered gravely. The confusion was written all over face. She could hear her heart beating faster. The content of the letter had slightly scared her. She clenched the ends of the paper in her hand, rushed back to the first word, and read the whole thing again. The letter still meant the same. She stared at the driver while the paper was left frozen between her fingers.

Henry, from the distance, could read the visible discomfort in her stare. He wasn't surprised and rather was expecting it. Especially after the distinct orders from his employee and the stern tension in Edward's voice while dictating Henry his task. Nevertheless, he felt it suitable not to appear to notice.

After spending several numb seconds at the door, Martha went back inside the house. For almost half an hour, Martha battled with her mind for a decision. She even peeped through the window several times to check if Henry had left – he hadn't. In fact, she did not like the idea of a man standing outside her house like a guard watching over a prisoner, threatening her personal space.

Martha, after spending a quarter of an hour, finally came out of the house and stopped at the porch. Henry hurried to catch her word as demanded. The moment he reached the steps of the porch; Martha stretched her hand and produced the same envelope before his face.

"Please hand this to Mr. Woods," she said plainly.

Henry was a little perturbed to see the same envelope being returned. Nevertheless, he obeyed and took the envelope from her.

"Any messages for Mr. Woods?" he questioned leaving no scope of complaints or disappointments from his end.

"No, that would be all," Martha replied with the same coldness.

"Have a good day, Madam."

He nodded his head in a hospitable gesture and left.

***

Henry wondered about Edwards's reaction on his way back to the Woods Residency. After providing eight years of service, and knowing Edward too well, he knew that his employer would be highly disappointed with the return of the letter. He did not know what message was scribbled on these pages, but he knew it was of much importance to Edward.

Edward was resting on the rocking chair in his library. The lights were dim. Only a single yellow fluorescent bulb was switched on lighting the three rows of the bookshelf enduring the weight of almost a hundred books. A burning cigar was fixed between his fingers and he was lost in his thoughts. The moment he heard footsteps entering the library, he immediately turned. Seeing Henry, he questioned him promptly.

"Did you meet Mrs. Edment?"

The anxiety in his voice made Henry hesitant to deliver the not-so-thrilling response.

"Yes, Sir, I did. She asked me to give you this." Henry offered the same envelope.

"What!! She returned it?"

Edward snatched it from his hand, got up, and headed for his reading table feeling completely troubled. He threw the letter on the reading desk and sat on the chair lowering his head over his hands looking exhausted. The tension started to develop again. He inhaled deeply and then stared from the corner of his eyes to question Henry again.

"Did she say anything else?"

"No, sir, I asked Mrs. Edment for any messages for you, to which she replied – No, that would be all."

Edward sighed in displeasure.

"You can leave now."

"Good afternoon, Sir." With that, Henry left.

After the pleasant meeting with Martha at the party and her much interest in his work and him, he expected her to be easily approachable. However, it did not turn out as expected. He leaned back on his chair and his shoulders slouched tiresomely. His eyes were set at the ceiling. Edward began to contemplate the situation, wondering in what other ways he could reach her, but then the volcano of emotions failed him, making it difficult for him to think straight.

He stretched his hand and picked the letter lying rejected and useless. He pressed his eyes and then opened the fold. The moment he slid out the letter, unexpected happened. Another piece of paper emerged and tumbled over the floor. Edward stared at it and eagerly bent to pick it. He fastidiously opened it and there he found words scribbled. His hopes returned at the mention of his name on the first line.

Mr. Woods,

I read your letter, but I have nothing to say as of now. Tomorrow, 1:00 PM, I will see you at your residency. No need to send your chauffer. I would come there on my own.

Regards

Martha

The instant Edward finished reading the note, a flicker of hope made itself evident through the resurrected eagerness in his eyes. Martha did not disappoint him and he was happy to know that. However, he also knew that this meant the beginning of an ordeal, because now he had to prepare himself to narrate some very distant memories. He was terrified even to remember them and this realization drew a silent fear inside him.

CHAPTER TWELVE

The road turned on a narrow path that went up the hill. Martha was seated inside the cab and felt her body drown against the car seat. She turned to look outside. A faint image of a church appeared, engulfed in the cold mist that usually follows after the rains in the hills. While she checked the knot of her woollen muffler, she noticed a cemetery just next to the church. In the silence and solitude of the place, Martha could hear the sound of water rushing in a river nearby, adding to the melancholy of the cemetery.

The hill divided Lanthom Cove into two different terrains – one to the left of the hill and the other to its right. Edward lived in the right half of the town and Martha had never been to that part of Lanthom Cove. She did not say anything to David, not just yet, not until she understood the gravity of the situation. For David, she was meeting an acquaintance from the dinner at Dylan's, and he was only glad to know this. He made the necessary arrangements of a cab that arrived just on time.

Passing the church, she checked her watch. She was right on schedule. Since the time she received the letter, Martha had tried to keep her calm, stopping her mind from creating narratives that persuaded Edward to write to her personally. But it was hard to ignore the blatant urgency in the tone of his letter. His words also suggested that in some way, it was also related to his profession. She only wondered what that meant. It further kept fuelling unsettling thoughts.

Finally, the Woods Residency came into view. Not only Martha, but the driver was equally surprised to see the expanse of the residence and how luxuriously it was built. The cab driver pressed the button of the electronic device fixed beside a massive iron gate and a woman answered gracefully.

"Who is it?"

Martha leaned forward towards the window and spoke.

"This is Martha Edment."

"Please come in."

The gates opened automatically. The cab drove in and stopped in front of the house under a massive bulk of a porch. Martha found a woman, who might have been in her late forties, neatly dressed, and who also looked well-mannered, to receive her. Her stern hospitable attire indicated that she was likely to be the caretaker of the residency than the mistress

"Good afternoon, Mrs. Edment. I am Donna Wilson, pleased to meet you."

The woman was charming and she gave Martha a pleasant smile that made her feel so welcomed.

"Good afternoon, Ms. Wilson."

"I hope it wasn't much trouble finding the place?"

"No, it wasn't. The driver knew the location well."

Donna slightly bent to her left, saw the cab, and made some more small talk.

"The town is quite just-enough in comparison to big cities. The locals are quite well versed with the routes in here."

Yet again a remark on how small Lanthom Cove really was. Everybody seemed to repeat it in some or the other way. Martha just responded with a smile. Her apprehensions did not allow her to be evenly social.

"I look after the running of the residency. Mr. Woods is expecting you in his library. Please come with me."

Martha followed while Donna leaded the way. They crossed an impressive drawing room that narrowed into a broad hallway. Edward was in the library that was built around the view of a flourishing garden. Martha felt a sudden peak in her anxiety, something that you feel just before addressing a dreaded moment. She didn't know how to address him. After all, they weren't meeting for an afternoon lunch to get better acquainted. This felt like meeting your doctor who had categorically asked you to see him in his clinic to discuss a critical health report.

The door to the library was halfway open allowing a stream of yellow light to enter into the dim hallway. Most of the house was also sadly dim. It wasn't the best welcome to alleviate her apprehensions.

Donna knocked on the door of the library.

"Come in," a grim voice answered.

"Mr. Woods, Mrs. Edment is here," Donna announced entering the library.

Edward was seated in his chair. His hands were clenched below his chin and elbows on the table. He was in this room but his mind was miles away. But at the mention of Martha, he immediately turned his head and stood alert on his feet.

"She has! Where is she?" he questioned fervently.

Donna displayed her surprise noticeably at his reaction. Edward felt a rush of embarrassment and calmed himself.

"She is right here, sir..."

Martha crossed the entrance of the library. Edward and she exchanged glances. He straightened his spectacles, and cleared his throat.

"Hello, Mr. Woods," Martha spoke stepping in further.

"Good afternoon, Martha."

They exchanged a few more awkward glances.

"Please have a seat," Edward said pointing towards a couch, not knowing what else to say.

"Would you like to have coffee, Mrs. Edment?" Donna offered.

Edward was coursing towards his desk, but stopped and turned at Donna half attentively. It was his duty to offer his guest. But he would have remembered about such necessities only if it had any importance next to the agenda of this meeting.

"Yes, Donna, coffee would be just fine."

He diligently began to shuffle through the rows of books after Donna left. The man who carried a very cheerful attitude in the party looked very solemn now. After a few minutes of silence and a thorough search of something in particular, Edward returned and sat on the couch opposite to Martha's. He carried a brown & shiny hardcover book that seemed to carry an important and rich text within its pages.

Martha ran her hand through her hair anxiously. She could not help but notice the strange objects displayed in the library. These were the ones you could easily spot in movies based on dark occult practices. On a nearby table was stationed a bulky volume titled as *Keepers of Inferno*.

"Gifts from people who appreciate my work; tokens of gratitude you can say," Edward spoke noticing Martha's discomfort at the sight of the assortment. "Some people feel that I have done a fair job in presenting the right picture of the supernatural. These objects represent the symbolic importance of their respective works."

Martha gave an assuring smile and nodded. Edward opened the book in his hand and began to read a verse.

Gods descend for the mortals,
When the hell rises to their very lands,
For the man shall keep its sane,
Or bid losing the only thing he can – his soul.

Martha stared at him wondering if it was her turn to speak. But she rather waited for Edward to continue.

"This is a verse from a book written some two thousand years ago. Do you understand it, Martha?"

"No, not really," she replied politely.

"It says that the only way a man can save himself from the clutches of the evil is by guarding his sanity, whatever it takes. And here the word evil is not used metaphorically, but instead, literally –" he hesitantly shifted his eyes from the pages of the book to Martha and finished, "– and by sanity, it points towards not losing your mind."

His voice had conviction and zeal for which he spoke further.

"Mind, something around which my research is based, in the context of supernatural. However, it surprises me that the strongest defence paranormal studies could outline after potential comprehension and decades of research was already written down by an anonymous man long ago."

Martha couldn't understand the context but pretended to be a good listener. She didn't know his intentions, that Edward wanted to build some base before he revealed to her what he wanted to. But Martha was reticent, and he knew he couldn't reach her, not just yet. A silence lingered between them for several seconds. When he realized that it was too early to anticipate a response, Edward finally questioned again.

"How much do you believe in supernatural, Martha? The existence of something unknown, breeding beyond the boundaries of our mortal world."

The skies grunted and a twig from a nearby tree knocked on the window. It caused a distraction and only after a few more seconds did Martha realize that Edward had asked her a question. She flipped her eyes hastily and brought them back in the library. It was her turn to speak and she searched for the right words to begin.

"I like to know about it," she finally answered.

"That's not what I asked."

"I mean..."

"Knowing about something and believing in it are two different aspects. Do you believe in the existence of supernatural?"

She found his tone interrogatory and that made her uncomfortable.

"Not much," she said firmly fixing a stern eye at Edward for the first time since she entered the room.

"You still aren't clear with my question."

The speech lacked its softness. In fact, it was rather strict, not out of superiority but a need to establish conciseness.

"No!" she started agitatedly this time but then instantly calmed down. "I mean... I am not saying that it is not true. Maybe I am yet to experience anything that could make me believe in it."

He stared at her remark – she had made a point. Just then they heard the sound of crockery. Donna appeared assisting a man who was carrying a trolley with a coffee set placed on it. The man halted near the center table and bent towards the crockery to serve.

"We'll serve ourselves. Thank you, Donna," Edward said indirectly asking his staff to leave.

Donna nodded at Edward, then to the man, with a noticeable difference in both the nods, who then placed the cup back on the tray and marched out accompanying Donna.

Edward waited for the door to close.

"Yes, personal tragedies do change one's beliefs indelibly."

"I didn't say tragedies, I said exper –" Martha tried to contest.

"But aren't tragedies experiences too, harsh ones." Edward cut her short.

She could hear a change in his breath, it was slightly faster, as if a silent fear suddenly made itself audible through the deadness of the library. Martha felt as if the room had become darker than it was. The light outside had become duskier too. Edward's rebuttal was effective. Martha had nothing else to say but to agree with him this time.

"Yes," she replied.

It was not the first time for Edward, to be sitting before the owners of unusual houses, battling with their doubt and fear, and sometimes ignorance and disbelief of one or more in the discussion. But this one was critical. Was it because this time he knew how it felt? Because this time he was one of the victims of the house in question?

He stood up and crossed the couch. He did not dare to look at Martha in the eye, fearing that it might weaken him in taking the leap that he had prepared himself for. He grabbed his cigar and he stopped at the window to light it. Having the capacity to change someone's fate comes with a certain responsibility. But this one also came with the horrors of revisiting a much-feared past.

It isn't about me anymore; it is now about her. She must know.

"Mr. Woods, your letter?" Martha questioned reluctantly. It was now time to talk about it.

Edward felt the heat rise around his ears. A few pinches of sweat appeared on his forehead. He took a long deep breath and finally began to speak.

"It was the fall of 1976 and I can still recall the images of that night, as if it all happened yesterday. It was the night which pushed me into something I never wished for..."

Martha silently followed his words while Edward had already slipped into a distant past.

I

9th June 1976,
West Hill Cove High School,
Lanthom Cove.
8:10 PM, Saturday

1976, it was the freshmen night at the West Hill Cove high school. One could smell the occasion from a distance. It promised something exciting already; rich with glamour and youth, the spell was such, leaving everything and everyone occupied enough to not notice the escape of three young boys from the driveway behind the school. With their veins drenched in booze, fear was not even the last thing that could stop them. Paul, the silly one of the three, took the challenge of breaking into his dad's garage and stealing his old truck for the night. Wesley drove the vehicle as he was the only one who could convincingly fool Edward, the cautious one, that he was sober enough to manage his hands on the steering.

The three musketeers, that's what they called their team, were so intoxicated that a passing cop could have easily charged them for life if they were caught. This momentary courage induced by alcohol also worked against their good judgement when they decided to break into the premises of the territory that was restricted and neglected for decades now.

"Look at that old piece of shit – here we come, Barcaldine!" Paul hooted at the sight of the house from the approach road.

Wesley stomped on the breaks right on time, just before the face of the rotten iron gate marking the entry of the property grounds. A few minutes later, they were in the premises they shouldn't have been on in the first place – they were soon to realize why not!

"It's not moving," announced Wesley in a stiff voice when the main door of the house, beyond the grand porch, refused to move at all even when he pushed with all his mettle.

"Let's break-in from one of the windows," said the geeky Paul who could not even keep his feet in one place.

It took Wesley one massive punch to shatter the glass that already hung loose from the frame of one of the windows. He jumped over the sill and fell heavily on the other side. He did not feel any pain but his head whirled. After him Edward got inside, carefully holding Paul, who, Edward knew, needed a hand even if Paul didn't want to admit it. Edward could smell the musty air of the house, and it caused irritation in his nose. There was an abandoned couch in the room they had broken into. It must have been the living room. Seeing it Paul could not control his cheesy humour even though he knew well enough that no one else would found it funny.

"What a fucked-up couch! I should get Karen here and give her a fuck or two on it," barked Paul into the silence. He pounced on it and started bouncing his dick against the cushion while faking an orgasm.

"Oh, shut your mouth, Paul! Keep your voice low! You have already made enough noise. We shouldn't get caught or I am grounded even before the first semester ends." Edward frowned. His tongue slipped every time he tried to speak. Alcohol did not go well with him and sadly his friends did not go well without it.

Paul obeyed, rolled his eyes, and ducked his lips like a foolish school kid.

Wesley produced the left-over vodka from his jacket and began to gulp it neat. His throat burnt but the high was too strong to feel any other heat except the one gearing around his pants.

Edward snatched the bottle from his mouth.

"Leave some for me too, you moron!" Edward couldn't stop laughing.

"And me too..." muttered Paul from somewhere around the couch foreseeing his future encounter with his girlfriend Karen.

Edward gulped the rest of it taking large sips and being fully aware that he was going to regret it in the morning. Nothing was left for Paul now. Edward knew Paul was already quite high and if another sip made through his mouth, he was bound to fall like dead meat.

The neat vodka hit like mercury rising under fire and Edward squeezed his eyes to surpass its pungent taste. Paul jumped at Edward to claim his share. They fell on the ground together tearing the bottle into numerous brittle pieces.

"Get off me, you bum! Wesley, get Paul off me!" Edward screamed in irritation. Even though Paul was lanky, he weighed heavier than he looked. It had something to do with bone weight as he once told them.

"Yeah... jj-just a minute," Wesley replied from somewhere inside the house. He wasn't in the same room anymore and wandered inside the house looking for a place to solace his bursting bladder. He made it to one of the vacant rooms, unzipped his pants hurriedly, and began to pee.

"Get away, Paul. You are fucking heavy."

Edward looked around with his dizzy eyes. He could barely feel any strength in his hands after the last shot. With the support of the wall, he struggled to stand on his shaky legs.

"Wesley, where the hell are you?" Edward called again.

Suddenly, a loud thrashing sound broke the silence of Barcaldine. It startled both Paul and Edward and shook them as if an electric shock ran through their veins. It left them silent, but alarmed. They squinted into the dark hallway to spot anything that could explain the reason of that noise.

"What was that?" Paul said.

"Wesley, are you all right?" Edward called again.

Their hearts thumped loudly. They knew their situation was critical; they were in a deserted house, everything was dark and abandoned, and lastly, they were too drunk to control anything if something unplanned happened. And just then, like before, another sound filled the house. This time they were sure that a window broke in one of the rooms.

Edward panicked and grabbed Paul's hand. He searched through the darkness looking for Wesley. His mind drew an unpleasant picture of Wesley seriously hurt and with that, he began to tremble. Paul was no less frightened. He feared to go beyond the dark hallway, not knowing where it would lead. They toppled and yet moved forward. The thrashing turned louder and frequent now. It was time for action. Edward sped up and ran into a curtain of cobwebs. It stuck to him like a fish caught under net. He tried to scratch it off from his face and when he opened his eyes, he saw Wesley before him.

Wesley stood right in front of him, but little could Edward realize that it wasn't the Wesley he knew. His head was dizzy. Everything appeared shaky, distant, and surreal. When Edward's eyes adjusted to the darkness, he saw Wesley, holding an iron rod, and he seemed ready to attack. Before Edward could stop him, Wesly continued to thrash everything around him maniacally.

"Wesley!" Edward shouted hoping to stop him.

Wesley turned with a sudden twist of his neck and howled at Edward like an animal. His eyes looked ferocious, aimed at warning anyone or anything that tried to come in his way. His jaw seemed sharper too, some of his teeth shined almost like fangs. Whether it was real or merely an illusion, Edward couldn't know. Just then Paul appeared rushing from behind and saw Wesley. He was stunned to see Wesley aiming at Edward.

"Wesley!!... Dude, what the hell are −" Paul began.

But before Paul could finish, he was cut short when a log of wood came flying towards him. His eyes widened at the unexpected attack and he fortunately escaped to his left. Edward saw that the attacker wasn't Wesley; both of his hands were tightly clasped around the rod. Then who aimed at Paul? But to his horror, no one else was visible to blame for those assaults.

This time Edward rushed to Wesley to stop him. He lurched and got hold of his arm. Wesley turned and groaned at Edward. Edward felt Wesley pushing his alcohol-breath out of his nose like an irked animal. The scorn on his face was filled with contempt. He was not the Wesley Edward knew, his eyes read something else, some other personality.

"What is the matter with you, Wesley, leave the damn rod!" Edward shouted at him.

At this, suddenly Wesley stopped and began to look into Edward's eyes, deeply, as if he aimed to hypnotize him. His breathing seized altogether and he drew a spiteful grin at Edward. Before Edward could understand that evil trick, a sudden burning sensation vaporized around his neck. It started as a light sizzle. But when he touched the back of his neck, he felt the heat gear up. There was no fire and yet his skin burnt severely.

"Ahhhh !!!" Edward screamed a short cry.

Before the sensation could intensify any further, Wesley drew his rod and hit Edward with immense force. The force of the blow was impossible to be drawn by the hand of an ordinary person. Edward flew all the way across the kitchen and crashed on the wall. The unbearable pain told him that he suffered a fatal injury. The red pool beneath him expanded with blood running out from his twisted and cracked ribs. He lay at a corner shivering like a slaughtered animal.

Wesley was not behind Edward; he wasn't in his sight anymore. But by the shadows fluttering on the wall, his actions were visible, and Wesley appeared like a demented vengeful criminal. The play of the shadows continued and Edward saw the silhouette outlining Paul who was now moving towards Wesley.

"No.... Paul...," Edward tried to warn Paul. But his voice was almost like a whisper and insignificant in front of all the thrashing and growling behind him.

And then came the unimaginable, suddenly he saw one more shadow manifest out of nowhere. A figure emerged from the wall behind Paul and took a defined but ghastly shape. It tore the wall and fell on the floor. It began to crawl like a wounded animal, but only it was not an animal, it was a large woman. The figure crawled slowly and deceitfully towards Paul. Her convulsive movements made the shadow appear even more dreadful. It was a nightmare. He wanted to warn Paul but his injured body failed him. Soon the woman clenched her fist around Paul's leg. Paul fell on the floor face down and let out a painful cry.

Nothing stopped Wesley from thrashing everything in his sight while Paul was being dragged away towards the wall. Paul's ghastly cries begging for help from Wesley, from Edward, replaced the deadly silence. Only his hovering echoes returned to him with no aid. Paul beat his hands and legs on the floor to free his body. He cried, screeched, and scratched the floor, but nothing could save him.

Edward began to weep silently, paralyzed by pain and fear. A grave regret took over him, regretting the decision of breaking into Barcaldine. It was only moments later when Paul disappeared into the same wall with the woman. In the end what remained of Paul were his cries of painful struggle echoing from somewhere inside the house. Even those cries couldn't bring Wesley back. He threw the rod and then began to hurt himself. He punched the window and his hand began to bleed. But it did not matter at all, something was demonstrating its anguish through him.

The violent noises began to go fainter to Edward's ears. His vision blurred and after losing a lot of blood, Edward passed out.

*

Present day,
Woods Residency,
Lanthom Cove.

Edward's silent sobs were intense but he steeled his heart to finish his narration. The cigar died untouched; coffee was left stale and cold.

"Five weeks later, I opened my eyes in special care after a brief period of coma, only to hear the worst," he wiped his tears hiding them from Martha.

"The cops found Wesley dead on the porch. The investigators concluded that he jumped from the first floor. Jumped or killed? Who knew? Deep wounds on his body and his own fingerprints suggested self-harm. The case was closed marking it to be an intentional jump, catalysed by alcohol and possibly undiagnosed depression, even though it was far from the truth. Wesley could have never ended his life. He was a happy man, one who looked forward to the future. I know that for sure. He was my friend." he said.

"The cause of Paul's death was transparent. Cops found him inside the house sitting beside my unconscious body; Paul had gone insane by then. He was admitted to the mental institution where he attempted suicide three times by hanging himself but was saved each time."

Those images came alive as if he could gaze into the distant and it was all happening right now before him.

"When Paul was stopped from harming himself, he pleaded for several nights, screaming that a voice commands him to do so. That was all he spoke after that night inside Barcaldine, until one morning he disappeared from the asylum. Police could not find his whereabouts for weeks until his corpse was discovered hanging near the river on a tree."

Martha felt her veins crawl beneath her flesh. What she felt was not just horror, it was something much deeper, a regret over a life gone wrong, with no hope of revival or recovery.

"Until the time I revived, Paul was the only potential suspect found at the scene. However, my return changed the facts that the investigators had drawn, for their convenience, claiming Paul to be the assaulter."

"I challenged the conviction of the investigators diligently. My statement seemed absurd. The cops wanted to believe me; I could see it in their eyes. They were the first witnesses of the actual scene before it was trimmed and suited for the public. Paul was not the culprit and they knew that well. No clues were found implying the assumption either."

Edward walked back to his desk; he heaved on the chair like a tired old man. It was the first time, in a long time, that he had narrated the entire event to someone. Martha was left frozen on the couch like a motionless rock being mercilessly hit by violent tides. Indeed, his words felt so to her core. She lost the track of time while the unspoken life of Barcaldine was confessed to her. It wasn't just any house now, it was her Barcaldine, the house of her dreams.

"Paul was also a victim; they all knew that well. Investigators were just doing their job; they were required to present a valid explanation. My statement suited their humour and seemed even beyond consideration. It was simply a breach of absurdity, as they called it. Nobody questioned them when Paul was declared responsible for

Wesley and me, an attack initiated after a brief quarrel on a drunk night, leading one thing to another. They refused to depend on my memory too. Neither Paul could stand in his own defence, who suffered his last days in an asylum," Edward said remorsefully. "Soon the case was closed, with the investigators' report, and sadly none of it was true."

He breathed deeply.

"I sometimes wonder how I made it alive from Barcaldine. May be because I collapsed before it could make me witness my own death like Paul and Wesley."

None of them spoke for the next few minutes and only the fright brought by the past did the rounds in Martha's head. At last Edward turned to face Martha and warned her, "Leave that house, Martha. This is not the home you want for your family. They will never be safe inside it."

CHAPTER THIRTEEN

"If my words still linger under the shadow of doubt, go and check the cemetery behind the church. You must have seen one on your way here. Wesley and Paul lie under their graves, their end marked by that unfortunate year," Edward spoke when Martha was leaving the library.

Martha did not utter a word afterwards, but Edward knew she was in shock. And anyway, what could she have said? or what had she not? But the fright of the moment barred her speech entirely. It wasn't easy for Martha, and nor to her boundary of beliefs. But above all she was also human with family, fears, and weaknesses, and Edward had twisted her world in an hour's time.

Edward did not persuade her for a response. But after she left, he did feel a strange guilt of passing the burden of his fears to her.   He had accepted his misery, but for Martha, there was still hope for an escape.

Emotionless tears ran down her cheeks as the car headed back to Barcaldine. She was neither exactly sad nor typically frightened. To her best conclusions, she was numb. When she ought to feel terror like any other person, Martha felt mentally tormented.

Edward was drunk, what if he had imagined everything? What if the cops were right? What if Edward was wrong? She thought aimlessly but then Edward's words echoed in her head and she felt goose bumps thrust on her skin. She did not refute his story. She remembered his ghastly face afterward, but suspicion always took the best of her and so was playing its role now.

Being a lawyer after all, her brief practice had taught her few handy details. However, supernatural presence or not, she wasn't fine with the fact that the end of two people was brought in her house.

"Stop at the church," she asked the cab driver who could pretty much feel her unease from the front seat.

"Sure."

Martha stepped down from the cab and headed towards the iron gate of the cemetery. The chill in the air was freezing and she pocketed her hands. Her cheeks, that had gone wet and cold, burnt in the air. She pushed the huge iron gate but did not step inside right away. Instead, she stood there for a while, feeling reluctant to move further. What difference would it make? She thought. Finding the graves will only worsen everything. Martha was somewhat sure of Edward's narration, at least the death part.

Looking at this enduring land, she realized that her story was now entangled with two deaths that lay beneath this ground. A cemetery which had nothing to do with her only hours ago held the answer she was looking for. Nevertheless, curiosity is a capricious feeling, it does always win intelligent reasoning. With that, Martha stepped in.

She wrapped her arms around her as if to shield herself from the dead underneath. She was the only visitor there at this hour. At one far end she saw a man wearing a robe standing outside the church gate. This did develop a sense of protection on her part. Martha walked across the narrow path and began to check the names engraved on various tombstones. The flowing fog revealed names as she walked closer.

Judith Downing
1904 – 1952
No

Austin Dougherty
1927 – 1978
No

Abbey Fabro
1945 – 1947
Oh, dear lord...

Jack Beckinsle
1934 – 1988

Trisha Karner
1967 – 2006

Addison Grith
1927- 1989

Martha could not locate the names she was looking for. There were about a hundred of them but still she did not give up.

Ryan foster
1951 – 2004

Eddison Grimshaw
1934 – 1999

Jeffery Heyne
1961 – 2009

She reached the foot of a statue of mother Mary with Jesus in her arms. This brought no solace to the surroundings but only added to its existing gloom. Her heartbeat ran faster now and she rushed her steps to look for more names. The sound of water dashing in the lake nearby sounded denser to her ears than it should have had.

Martha hurried. An anxious feeling began to fill her chest.

Henry Swoth
Madison Gltih
Rebecca
Timothy
Stevenson
Gri..
Del...
Wes..
Ros..
Gabri...
Doroth...
Philip

Martha halted abruptly. She checked something from the corner of her eye. Her steps took a backward roll and she began to read the row backwards.

Philip
Dorothy
Gabriel
Rose

Wesley Kendall

4th October 1955 – 7th June 1976

The clouds rumbled. The wind hit the bell tower swinging the bell around its iron hook. The bell sounded as if it drew a large moan. Martha's eyes were stuck on those letters and numbers confirming what she came here to know. The inscription flashed before her eyes radiantly as if no other grave existed, and she was right – it did not make anything better.

The man in the robe followed her every move, but even his presence could not calm the outbreak she felt gearing up. She read the date again and it still read the same.

Wesley and Paul still rest under their graves; the words were stamped legit now. Unable to deal with it any further, Martha suddenly turned and ran back for the cab. The gate was around twenty graves away and she burst towards it as if a hand from beneath would bulge out to get her as she once dreamt when she was ten.

She didn't need to check another slab hiding Paul's decomposed corpse. This was enough!

CHAPTER FOURTEEN

"Who told you?”

“What?”

He dropped the spoon and questioned agitatedly. His half-eaten food lay cold on the plate.

“Who told you about this?” David questioned demandingly this time.

“Why are you getting so angry? Isn’t it good that I got to know about it?”

“You were not supposed to know,” the words slipped from his tongue and he regretted saying it right away.

“You knew about this?” Martha began in shock.

She stared at David and he looked back at her with guilty eyes. In an instant, he dropped the adamant face he was holding onto.

“You knew about it, David?” Martha repeated accusingly this time.

He sighed away heavily.

“Did you?” she repeated loud enough this time to make him feel even guiltier.

He pushed back his chair and stood up. Lifting his plate, he turned to march towards the sink and run away as far as he could from this conversation.

“Tell me, David!”

“Yes, I knew it.” he muttered in a suppressed bitter tone. He rigorously scrubbed the leftover from his plate, facing his back to her.

"What!" Martha was swept away with disbelief, "Since when? Who told you?"

"I own this house, what made you think I didn't know?"

"And you didn't care to tell me?"   Martha felt cheated and the look she drew at him conveyed her feeling of betrayal.

"It's no big deal, Martha. Some drunk kids broke into an abandoned house and suffered an accident – what was there to tell?"

"I cannot believe you! No big deal! You decided to settle us here and you did not even care to tell me the whole truth." She thumped her right hand furiously on the table. "goddamnit, look at me."

"Would you have agreed to come here if I had told you? Huh? Tell me, Martha?" he turned and finally faced her this time. He hurried to the next shelf and snatched the hanging cloth to wipe his hands.

"And anyhow, people die in every house, and that doesn't make them any less adaptable. I protected you from unnecessary worry, but it seems you love trouble." He had never spoken to her so repulsively, nor Martha took it well.

"What?? I'm not some six-year-old who doesn't understand this. But at least I deserve to know the truth, David. You can't just make stuff in your head and hide things from me."

"Argh! Martha! Don't make an issue of it, please! It's not like I attempted murder, and moreover I can see how positive you are about this revelation."

"I would have taken it rationally if I hadn't got to know about this from outsiders when I could have had from my own husband!"

David immediately relaxed. He realized there was no point in fighting over this. He was wrong. He dropped the cloth in his hand and calmly walked towards her.

He held her shoulders and turned her to face him.

"Ok, listen, I am sorry. I should have told you. But please understand, I was worried about you. This was the only place where I could start a new life, and I thought you might not agree to come if I had told you about that incident. My intentions were not to hurt you at all."

Martha's eyes were low, staring at the floor. She began to scratch the table top which she usually did whenever she was tense. She jerked her shoulder where David put his hand and showed her further disapproval.

"Martha?" he called her for a reply.

She did not say anything.

"I hope you are not getting superstitious?" David said worriedly.

"Come on... No, David, I am not!" she turned towards the chair releasing his arm. "I am not thinking anything that absurd," she told him so even though she remembered vividly every bit of Edward's version. "But it's a hard fact to live with. Some boys died here, in our house, it is complicated." She had pacified a little by now and displayed worry more than anger.

"Martha, people die in every house, and if you see, this was an accident. I agree it was very unfortunate. But, in the end, it was an accident."

He might have also doubted his deductions only if he had heard what Edward had to tell.   She was in a dilemma. What was the truth? The lines were blurring.

"By the way, who told you about this?" David questioned hoping that she would reply to him evenly this time.

She raised a determined look at him and said,

"Remember the paranormal researcher I met at the party? Mr. Woods?"

"Yes,"

"He was one of the victims; the only one who survived out of the three."

"What? Oh my god, how do you know?"

"I met him."

"When?" David questioned her quickly, but it barely took him a second to guess the answer for the same.

***

Some more time passed in the house after her meeting with Edward. Those ghastly memories and that silent testimony of the facts in the graveyard began to grow somewhat distant. Nothing happened in the house that could make way for suspicion. Maybe David was right; she began to agree half-heartedly. David's constant ridicule towards anything superstitious helped in cementing what he wanted Martha to believe.

Did the house have a mind of its own? If Martha knew the entire truth, only if she had believed what Edward said, she would have known that the house chose to retrieve for now, like a lion hiding in its den, waiting for the prey to grow more vulnerable.

CHAPTER FIFTEEN

Ben felt frequent headaches in the mornings. This had been going on for a week now. It was worrisome because this wasn't normal for a kid of his age. This left him sleep deprived and it was concerning now. The cold that generally geared up around two in the night was unbearable. Every night he managed to fight the chill only after closely tucking two blankets around his body. However, to his surprise, sometimes the room felt warmer than the season allowed, and there would not be any need of a blanket. Later, the same night, he would again find himself shivering around four with cold bumps all over his skin.

He complained to his father about this, he believed there was a fault with the central heating system. At times, it pushed more air than required and sometimes none at all. After all, the system was old, just like the house itself. However, David never found any faults to fix; it was working just fine. Ben inquired Susan to know if she faced any similar challenges. Susan had now shifted to a separate room because she hated sharing one, and unlike her brother, she was extremely satisfied with it.

That morning, Susan was particularly excited about the camp her school had organized for the following week. She was looking forward to it and had planned to talk to her parents about this over breakfast. A similar trip was set for Ben's batch and so he was equally keen, but instead, he chose to start the conversation with a less exciting invitation.

"Mom, can I sleep with dad and you? I just can't sleep in my room," Susan writhed her face at Ben, feeling offended at being cut off by him when she was about to speak.

"Why, Ben, what happened?" Martha questioned.

"My room is cold. I cannot sleep in there. The heater in my room doesn't work."

"It isn't fixed yet?" Martha turned to David who sensed it coming, "David, didn't you check it yet?"

"I did, but couldn't find any faults," he answered in his defence.

"Then call someone who can."

"Fine, we'll get it checked. You can sleep with your sister till then," David exhaled noisily and replied.

"Dad! I am not going to share my room," Susan protested even before the deal was closed.

"Susan, you better behave like an elder sister and cooperate with your brother," Martha snapped at her. Susan did not dare to argue further and risk her trip.

"Ok, dad, I will." She lowered her face and grumbled.

Before anymore burden could come on her, Susan rushed with her news.

"Mum, there is something I want to talk about. Our school has organized an educational camp on wildlife next week. It is a six-day trip and I really want to go. Please, can I go?"

"And me too. My batch is going too. I want to go too," Ben hopped in after Susan.

"Educational camp; well, that sounds like a good idea. Isn't it, David?" Martha began approvingly.

"Well, yes, it is," David answered rather plainly. He stood up to get some juice from the refrigerator.

"So, when do you kids leave?" asked Martha.

"On Wednesday, next week," Her answer was prompt.

"What about your batch, Ben?"

"Same day, I have a circular you can check,"

He fastidiously searched the contents of his small bag and produced a slightly wrinkled paper out of it.

"Here it is." Ben handed it obediently.

"Yeah, the Declaration form; stupid odd formality. I got one too," Susan said, "here you go, its crap - have fun!"

"It's not stupid, Susan. It is important so that kids like you stay within your limits while you are away from your parent's vigilance," David said sternly from behind.

"Do you understand what your father explained?" Martha added and smiled at Susan's over-smart attitude.

Susan rolled her eyes under her lowered head pretending to eat her cereal sincerely. Her hair fell to the sides which prevented Martha from seeing that added sarcasm. David sipped his juice while he leaned against the kitchen shelf. He remembered how he too nagged about these forms. It gave his parents a chance to recap the same old lecture about watching his behaviour in school, and which was usually fifteen minutes longer at the time of trips. Although the lecture never worked, he still returned with a long list of penalties.

"Martha, would you come here for a minute?," David called from behind.

Martha was going through the circulars, checking all the important details of the trip about food, travel, and security. Expense seemed affordable too.

"In a minute," she replied.

David left the kitchen to collect his bag.

"Well, it seems all good. Your dad and I will discuss it and do the formalities by tomorrow."

"Thanks, mom," Ben hugged Martha.

"That would be great, mom." Susan added.

"Now, hurry up and finish your breakfast. Otherwise, you will miss your bus."

Saying that, Martha left to speak to David.

David was clipping some papers. It was usual of him to rush for every corner of the house at this hour, looking for things that he always forgot where he kept them and mostly, they were of utmost importance. He always made a fuss when he could not find them as if others were to be blamed. Afterwards, he always gave that awkward smile feeling like a complete fool when his memory turned out to be the real culprit. Well, it was a mundane story now and Martha delayed her climb up the stairs leaving enough time for David to find his things before he threw up his child-like tantrums.

"You were saying something," she finally reached the door.

"Martha, yeah there was something," he said slowly.

He walked towards her silently with some papers in hand. He seemed calm but concerned.

"Are you sure about sending the kids for the camp?" asked David.

"Well, yes, it would be quite lucrative. Why, shouldn't we?"

"Hmm... yes, it is just that... umm... I was just –"

He scratched his right eyebrow trying to hide his hesitance.

"Actually, I forgot to tell you, I have this client with a civil case at hand, and he is in New York presently. Since I have worked in New York for a longtime, the firm wants me to look after the case."

"I see. But what does it have to do with the kids?"

"They want me to leave for New York and meet the client for a discussion. It is a big case from a close acquaintance of my boss. They are really counting on me and, I have to leave on Tuesday."

"So that's ok. Kids are leaving on Wednes –,"

"– I might not be back before the end of the week," he added before she could finish.

He touched the unstated worry. Lately, everything had been difficult enough and this meant Martha had to be alone for days with the knowledge of all that she knew and all that she was forcing herself to be calm about. Days were fine but could Martha go through the nights on her own? Night; the stimulator of all the natural human fears, even if they are only imaginary, yet they manifest under the shadows of the moon. Then one feels short of breath after sensing hidden demons approaching out of the dark and empty corners.

Martha dropped her projectile gaze on the floor, indecisive of how to respond. She understood what David meant. However, she did not want to let her fears paralyze her family's freedom. Work was important and it will not be the first time she would have to stay alone; she might have to deal with it in future too. Why not start from now, she told herself.

"David, I can stay alone. You don't have to worry about me," she looked straight into his eyes sounding confident and assuring.

He held her by her shoulders and came close. She felt cared for and protected.

"Martha, if you are not fine with it, I will ask the firm to postpone it."

She caressed his chest. His apprehensions were clear to her.

"No, you don't have to. I will be fine, trust me," Martha said reassuringly.

He kissed her and hugged her. His cologne was strong and she loved the fragrance. From above her chin resting on his shoulder, she gazed out of the window that opened straight into the old green branches of her backyard, and she prayed that her words would stand by her even when she is left alone with her house, with the mysterious Barcaldine.

CHAPTER SIXTEEN

The night before Tuesday was the hardest. David was to leave the next morning. Martha did hear a few unidentifiable sounds during late night that startled her but she did not react. They were just usual noises heard in every house. There is an explanation; I just don't know about it, she told herself.

Creaking sounds of moving hinges were frequent during the night. She was sure that it was most likely an open window rotating about its span. There was nothing to worry, except one thing; what was moving it? Next, she heard what sounded like someone was dragging the furniture followed by a loud thump just like the dropping of a hammer. But Martha told herself that all of it was passable. Her mom told her that she could hear them in her grandma's and uncle Barney's house too. Nobody knows what creates these noises, but you can sleep knowing that it is normal and can be disposed of, her mother had said. That learning certainly helped.

In the end, she wrapped her hand around David and slept letting the midnight battle of unrequited noises continue without an audience.

But the spectators kept their vigilance!

***

David held Martha by her waist and gave her a long kiss, the way she loved it. She could smell his fresh coffee breath that felt good. A light cold breeze was flowing all around and in his arms, she felt wonderful.

"You will be fine?"

"A millionth time – yes!" she replied.

"Hmm," he smiled.

He drew a long glance towards the house and its surroundings and noticed the sky curling into grey crumbles.

"The air seems different today – much stronger and thicker!" he said.

"Thicker?"

"– or is it just your love working its magic," he rubbed his nose with Martha's.

He kissed her again followed by a gentle hug. The sweet smell of her hair was still the same and reminded him of the first time he touched her.

"I'll miss you, baby," he said in her ear. Martha could feel the movement of his lips over her skin.

"I'll miss you too."

David got into the car and rolled the glasses down. The tires crushed the brown leaves that were shedding quite a lot lately. Their backyard was full of them and many more were likely to fall any time soon.

"Drive safely."

"Yes. I will call you. Take care."

The car skidded out through the front gate, drifting away bits of stones from its path over the sidewalks. It was drizzling now and he switched on the wipers to get a clearer view of the road ahead. He tuned his favourite Beatles album and rolled up the glasses to avoid the chill from getting to his tonsils.

CHAPTER SEVENTEEN

Ben stood under the porch with his small backpack and his chin inside the muffler coiled around his little neck. The woollen cap was also efficient in cutting the cold. Last night sleep with his mom saved him from an early headache. While he rubbed his palms to generate some natural body heat, he spotted Susan dragging her luggage out of the house. Ben's one quick look was enough to judge that stuffed baggage, more than it was required, and he came up with the right expression to convey his distaste at his sister's desperation. They were waiting for the hired cab to arrive and drop them to school. His mother was complaining from inside the house to Susan who pretended not to hear her by wheeling down the luggage noisily.

The sound of the crackling engine approaching towards the iron gates thickened.

"Mom, it's here," Ben shrilled in his yet-to-mature voice.

"Yes, I am coming," Martha answered.

Martha, upstairs in her room, slid her hand into the sleeves of her heavy long coat. Ben called again. The engine groaned before falling silent. She peeped through the window while her fingers rushed to button the coat and saw the cab driver dragging Susan's fat luggage. Martha grabbed her purse and was on the staircase when Ben called her for the third time.

She grabbed the keys of the house and just when she was about to reach the exit door, her phone rang. It must be David, she thought happily. She nailed the key into the keyhole to avoid forgetting it near the telephone. The phone had rang long enough and would disconnect any second. To avoid the same, she rushed to answer it.

"Hello," she was gasping.

"Martha, are you fine?" answered a worried voice.

"Who, David?" she asked quickly.

"No," the voice hesitated, "It is Edward."

A shudder went through Martha. His voice flashed all the scenes of the library in her mind like a movie playing on the screen.

"Hello ..." she finally said

"Are you alright? Why are you gasping?"

"Yes, I am fine. I was just hurrying to leave for somewhere."

There was silence again and then Martha was the first one to speak.

"What is the matter, Mr. Woods?" Martha indirectly questioned the reason of his call.

"I never heard from you again. I was a bit concerned, so I thought of checking on you," he replied.

Martha heard Susan calling her impatiently from across the door. She did not want to have this conversation again. She wanted to hurry before the kids came inside looking for her.

"We are fine, Mr. Woods. I have to go now... I am in a hurry; can I talk to you later?"

"Wait... Martha, did you see –" he began.

Martha felt a wave of tension rise in her head and this irked her. She knew he wanted to know about her visit to the cemetery and he need not complete his sentence to convey it.

"Yes, Mr. Woods, I did, and I don't want to talk about it!" she snapped back.

"What? Why? What happened, Martha? Wait, don't you believe what I told you?"

There was hostility in her speech and it feared Edward not of rejection but of her ignorance that she seemed to have had opted for. It took him less than a second to realize the developments, the evils of disbelief were not new to him.

"I never said that, Mr. Woods. But I confess that I do have my doubts."

She spoke her mind though her words lacked conviction. On the contrary, blurting out her mind made her doubt it even more.

"Martha, don't fall into this pit. For god's sake, please leave Barcaldine...."

He sounded ominously commanding. Instead of having the desired effect, it alarmed Martha.

"Mr. Woods, I-HAVE-TO-GO-NOW!," she said coldly.

Martha braced her tears, preventing them from escaping her eyes. She banged the receiver down. The miserable feeling returned.

"Mom, we are getting late," Susan called again. Martha heard her approaching. She quickly wiped the little moisture that had made it to her eyes.

"I am almost there," she answered back. It was strange but she felt a sudden loss of energy. She grabbed her purse and walked out. She closed the door behind and locked it without making any further delays.

Susan stood beside the open door of the cab and didn't notice anything strange when her mother numbly sat in the car. The engine roared again, puffed smoke towards

Barcaldine, and left.

CHAPTER EIGHTEEN

The vision never re-appeared after her visit to Barcaldine. Amie was relieved to gain the surety of herself, that she was fine, that she had not slipped into her old-self, and that nothing from her past was waiting with its claws open and fangs out. It was nothing, just a misjudgement, she had consoled herself by repeating this and in a few days the world around her stabilized.

Amie eagerly waited for Martha at a table in her favourite restaurant. This was her preferred spot, just next to the glass from where she could observe the narrow lanes undisturbed by the calm life of her town. The view from the The Crossing Inn had remained pretty much the same, at least since the time she had started going there as a teenager. The crowd never bothered her here. She never worried about her posture or how her fingers moved with the cutlery. She could just quietly sit there, enjoy her meals, and gaze at the world.

Martha pulled the entrance door and entered. She looked for Amie and spotted her. Amie still hadn't noticed Martha's arrival as she walked towards the table.

"Hello, Amie."

Amie turned her face and Martha was standing right in front of her.

"Oh, hello, Martha," she stood up and gave Martha a friendly hug.

Martha kept the dripping umbrella close to her side. Once they were settled, the owner felt relieved. Finally, there was to be an order. The waiter geared up to initiate the prospects of his tips; women customers were generally more generous than men.

"Warm place," Martha said, almost like a murmur.

"Yes, it's a very old restaurant. I love it."

Martha smiled dimly and crossed her arms on the table. She flipped her hair lightly and studied other people in the restaurant. To her comfort, their table was at a secluded corner. She could discuss what she wanted to, only if she managed to bring herself to the matter. Everybody around was pre-occupied with their own conversations, queries, issues or whatever that might be. What mattered was that nobody was eavesdropping.

"How are you, Amie?"

"I am fine. How about you?"

"Yes, I am fine too."

Martha's state of discomfort was not passable; Amie noticed it. Martha was not as enthusiastic as Amie expected her to be. They ordered coffee that was quickly serviced.

Martha was stirring the spoon into the heavy froth of her cup and didn't realize when Amie spoke.

"Huh? What?" Martha began, "I am sorry, did you say something?"

"Are you alright? You don't seem quite yourself today," Amie pressed her hand against Martha's in consolation.

There was no point in pretending that she was fine. Martha's mother always said that she was bad at faking moods. This only made her look even more stressed and Martha knew that was true.

"Umm. Yes, there is something," Martha said, "In fact I wanted to talk to you about it."

Amie moved forward to hear Martha closely. Her admittance made Amie grow even more concerned. Martha kept her gaze fixed at the coffee mug as she spoke.

"You have been in Lanthom Cove since your childhood, so you might know about this –" Martha stopped and looked around, everybody was engrossed as noticed earlier, but she still felt reluctant to go forward.

"What is it, Martha?" Amie persuaded.

"– Or probably you don't even remember it. It's been so long after all." And then she finally said it, "Well it is about a tragic incident that happened some thirty years ago. Some drunk kids who broke into –"

"– Barcaldine? Your house? Yes, I remember it. I was nine then. It shook the entire town.

"You remember it?"

"Yes, I do," she saw the look on Martha and added. "Oh no, I thought you knew..."

Martha lowered her head.

"No, I didn't. David never told me, in spite of the fact that he knew about it all along. I somehow got to know a few days back," she said regretfully. She did not want to talk about Edward.

"I am so sorry, Martha. I would have mentioned only if I knew you weren't aware."

"No, it's not your mistake; you don't have to apologize."

"What led David to finally tell you this?"

"He didn't. I happened to meet someone at a dinner party who brought it up," she disclosed the bare minimum. There was no need to talk about visiting Edward. It wouldn't have helped in anyway. What mattered were the deaths. It is very unsettling to know that your house hold such painful memories. Were the reasons disputable enough to move out of Barcaldine? She didn't know and even if they were, where would they go? This came to their rescue when they were about to be homeless. But home meant safety, and somewhere Martha still believed that the house was harmless, even if it wasn't clean on papers.

"So, what is troubling you now, Martha?" questioned Amie unable to comprehend the problem.

Martha expected Amie to understand her situation without her having to explain the details, but it didn't happen. It left Martha a little agitated.

"Amie... all the deaths! That is my problem," Martha blurted, and she realized right away that she was, in truth, more troubled about the series of events that led to those deaths.

So, she knows about all of them, Amie thought.

"What about the deaths, Martha? Look they happened decades ago. People die everywhere and it's just a simple fact that a few died in your house too. After all it's such an old house and has stood there for ages now. Things were bound to happen under its roof some way or the other."

Amie with her matter-of-fact tone sounded like David's apprentice. But this wasn't the worst of it, because Martha didn't know yet that Amie was referring to more than what Martha understood. None of them knew that they hung on different strands of Barcaldine's history.

Amie looked around; nobody was peeping at them, eavesdropping or showing any slightest questionable interest. Amie could also continue now.

"Martha, I lost my grandfather, mother, and my uncle in this very house I live in. It wouldn't make it any less homely for the next owners if I ever wish to sell it," Amie added with sincerity. Her struggle in her early years had made her significantly tuned with the actuality of life. She might have had a vague persona now, but the command of her speech was unmatched. Amie reminded Martha of law students who looked so imperfect to be lawyers. However, when they opened their mouths, they blew away everyone.

"You are right. Maybe I am just a bit shocked. All this has come as a surprise to me. May be if I knew before I moved here, I would have had time to accept it."

"It's better this way if you come to think of it. Otherwise, you would unnecessary trouble yourself with things that really don't matter."

"Maybe"

"Houses are demolished, rebuilt; towns are extended to cities. Who knows the history of every piece of land used? Moreover, everything goes just fine. So, isn't it better to not know anything and live in peace? I guess so, yes!" Amie compiled and fell back in her chair like one does after a long tiresome run.

Martha listened to Amie carefully and her words were able to console her afflicted mind. She also got tempted at times to narrate Edward's side of the story. After the call this morning, it was all coming back to her vividly.

Amie had been wanting to discuss something else too, especially now when their conversation was focused on those distant grave memories. She did not understand the need for this herself, but words seemed to be always hanging at the verge of her tongue when it came to Barcaldine. It was one of those things you liked to discuss because it was just exciting to talk about it, even though it did not change anything. Out of a similar urge, there were a few names that Amie was keeping shut in her mouth for a while now, but now felt suitable to blurt them out.

Amie slightly pursed her lips. She had a mischievous innocence in her eyes, and that too of a child who was feeling dubious whether to speak or not. She set her eyes on Martha who was staring deep into her cup with a look that reminded Amie of telepathic readers.

"In fact, the memories of the Willard family are completely non-existent now; I am surprised that you even heard about them. Wasn't expecting anyone to have slightest knowledge of it today," Amie said.

Just then, Amie felt her coffee needed some more milk and she signalled one of the waiters. Martha retrieved from her trance like state.

"Who?" Martha questioned.

The waiter poured milk into the cup and the ingredients turned from black to pale brown.

"The Willard family; I am sure David must have mentioned that name." Amie said, and then to the waiter. "Enough, no more, thank you."

The restaurant had become noisier than it was half an hour ago. By the time Amie was done suiting the coffee to her taste; she realized Martha was gazing at her with a confused-curious look. For a moment it seemed Martha would freeze in her chair if Amie did not prick life back into her by some interruption. The window behind Amie let in golden light from the skies for a fraction of a second. She could see Martha's age confided in her wrinkles.

"Willard, who?" Martha asked again stressing on the name.

The sound of her crisp voice had a curious note to it. Martha's lack of recognition towards the mentioned name was alarming to Amie. She felt a gulp down her throat when Martha's passiveness revealed her lack of knowledge. Amie caught the eye of the restaurant owner who had been behind the same desk from the last nineteen years. He still did not credit to her loyalty as a customer and neither was of any help to her to alter the course of her conversation now. The fear was not of the woman demanding answers, but the worry – will she be able to take it?

Amie could not hide the unpleasantness derived in her eyes looking back at Martha and Martha grasped it well. Amie demanded a walk till the gates of Barcaldine, she needed some time before wording out the memories of The Willards, and thereby unwrapping another lost decade in the life of Barcaldine, and this time from the beginning of it.

Martha unquestioningly walked out of the café after the bill was settled even though the coffee mugs were barely touched. The change in Amie was elusive, and yet Martha realized she was about to hear something that would affect her life and she was better off without knowing. A part of her warned her to guard herself against any more revelations and yet another steeled to endure further.

The route back to Barcaldine was one not known to Martha. It was a narrow track hosting sans human life on its either side. Amie informed that it was a straight road, back to Barcaldine. They came across only three houses at a stretch of a mile and on the rest stood the peripheries of the forest. The smell of the wet earth was persistent in the air here than it was ever known to be in any other part of Lanthom Cove.

"I would suggest that you don't ask for this, Martha. I must tell you; it won't make any difference," Amie said briefly, the decency in her voice was sincere.

Martha lowered her head and bit her lip slightly in consideration. But it was more of a silence conveying that she respected Amie's concern, but wasn't backing after all.

"I want to know," Martha said coherently. The assuring voice carried her painful curiosity behind it. Amie felt guilt for causing another hole in Martha's perfect world. Though, done unknowingly, it didn't help in alleviating the effect of her mistake.

They reached a rocky bench whose rough surface had cuts and cracks implying its age. The order of its arrangement indicated that it was a stoppage for bygone travellers of a forgotten time. It was barely long to seat three people at a time but enough for these two women to sit on. They settled on it.

Martha's yearning eyes were repeatedly stroking Amie to begin. Amie retrieved from her pensive state to draw the first words in introduction of an unspoken family in the history of Lanthom Cove.

"Willards – the first owners of the Barcaldine house," she started as if casting a mysterious spell, "the Willards of the Barcaldine mansion first arrived in Lanthom Cove in the year 1942. Among one of the very early British families that settled here, Mr. Daniel Willard was a wealthy man with a heart of gold. He was one of those typical English men with a perfectly justifiable wife beside him to embrace his goodness; Mrs. Willard indeed was known to be right for him. They had two daughters and a son that made the family complete, and a happy one too, before their misery began and slowly marked their end."

Amie inhaled deeply and glanced at the blue horizon.

"They say Mr. Willard's youngest daughter was not his own but of his brother. The girl was left to him after his brother died, who had already lost his wife at the time of childbirth. Her name was Emily, I remember it. She was known to be a silent girl, a very shy person. Emily was deprived of real parents, but it is said that Mr. and Mrs. Willard made sure to fill that void with best efforts and the family accepted her as their very own. Their children never had a problem either. It is known that Emily disappeared one day, she went out, and never returned."

Amie sighed on the fact and took a deep whispery breath.

"Nobody knows what happened to the poor girl. Days passed and after all the failed searches, it was concluded that she might have had lost her way in the forest eventually getting killed by a wild creature. They used to say that the forest ate her. Her body was never found either, but after a few weeks, her shoes and a few shreds of her clothes drenched in blood were found in the woods, which confirmed her death. This tragedy marked the beginning of the end of the Willards."

With each step into the past, her voice turned deeper, painful, and thicker.

"Mr. Willard could not take it well. Emily was very dear to him, more than anyone else, and he blamed himself for this. After bouts of depression and prolonged periods of melancholy, Mr. Willard died, he killed himself. After him, Mrs. Willard went numb. She refused to continue with life anymore. There were days when she would not gulp a grain down her throat. And to make things worse, Mrs. Willard began to discourage visitors into Barcaldine. It is believed that she lost her mind. People who came forward to console her, she insulted them with hoarse speech. Soon the town started dreading the Barcaldine completely. I suppose servants were fired too and nobody knew what was happening inside the house anymore. No one was ever seen stepping in or out of Barcaldine. The kids never left the house either; they were under house arrest by their mother. Days passed when the cops finally took the charge; Mrs. Willard needed help. After constant knocking on the door and much disappointment, they broke in."

The longest narration was interrupted by a hesitant pause. Her eyes seemed as if all of it was happening right now before her. Amie felt the intensity of her own words. Martha felt lost, unaware of what her world actually comprised of. Barcaldine, her own house, now appeared like a mysterious territory. It didn't sound like the past of her own house, because no part of her world could be related to such a brutal destiny. When Amie looked into Martha's eyes, the chill in them made way for the final note. The eyes had steeled for the conclusion.

"All three of them were found dead – Mrs. Willard went completely insane, murdered the last two bearers of her family, and then hung herself. The Willards were erased from the pages of time, forever."

The zeitgeist had appeared with the most unexpected this time, digging its paws up to the core. Martha frantically began to stare at the ground. The images of this new discovery began to beat like an undulating pain in her head, gaining shape and form inside her mind. Amie turned Martha to face her, providing her a secure frame to control her shaping hysteria.

"Martha! Do not assert to any of this more than required. Willards are long forgotten and they do not exist anywhere anymore."

She could see that Martha wasn't listening anymore. She was losing herself, slipping into that dreadful passage of time, rechannelled by the memories of the Willards. Martha looked calm but the frown above her eyes was intact. Amie shook her vigorously, grabbing her by her shoulders. Martha's head quivered over her narrow neck, as if she was lifeless, and then she looked at Amie.

"How do you know all of this?" Martha questioned. She had an indignant note in her speech. Amie felt a repulsion from her, but Amie knew that the repulsion was not aimed at her but at Martha's ignorance of the past.

"My grandfather worked for the Willards once, when he was quite young."

And the words struck like the final judgement in the courts of law. Amie made the fact legitimate enough. Martha let herself free from Amie's grip and ran the way back to her home. She couldn't stand it anymore. The only hope that it could have been a bizarre tale reported by the evils of speculation was also ruled out.

"Martha!!" Amie yelled from behind.

Amie wanted to run and follow Martha but she decided not to. Any other person in the same situation would have felt offended by Martha's unexpected reaction, but Amie did not, because it occurred to her that she might have had reacted in the same way, because like Martha, she herself was not comfortable in displaying her vulnerabilities. Amie watched Martha run farther away until she disappeared in the curving of the narrow road.

She thought it was better to leave Martha alone at the moment, that time would heal, and take care of the rest

***

Martha ran irrespective of any knowledge of how she would reach back home. She wanted to run away from all of it, from Amie, from Edward or anyone who was forcing cracks into her world. She ran noisily on the bed of autumn leaves, crushing them to dry ashes.

The passage had become darker under the shade of branches meeting like two large hands at the top. A slight wind embarked, whistling amongst the trees. Her breath grew heavy and yet she pushed her muscles further to take her away from the past, but it was ironic, because with every step she was only walking closer to it.

Her mind was painfully occupied. Her hands and ears had gone cold as she ran against the wind. The inside of her throat felt icy too. She finally noticed the course of the track when the back of a house appeared, and it was her own Barcaldine. Her body slowed down to an abrupt halt. A glade opened from the woods to the back of the house.

She looked at the house, which stood like a peaceful and beautiful shelter. Its features redone and refurbished did not suggest any air of mystery enveloping it. Fifteen minutes must have had passed when her cold stare softened with a hint of warmth for the house. Martha reviewed her life and recalled how she had made troubles look down before her unbeatable strength.

In between her attempts to reconcile with her faith, flashes from Edward's library, along with Amie's recent revelations tried to weaken her again. Martha could swear that a part of her brain tried to link the two narrations, but whenever she looked at the house, it surprisingly stood innocent to her. She came out of the dark glade and moved slowly towards Barcaldine recalling the first time when she approached the house from the car.

She wanted to call David, but what if he knew about this too? And if this was the truth, she couldn't risk feeling betrayed again. But at the same time, the need to drain out her frustration seemed indispensable. The last time David had called was yesterday. She hurriedly looked for her cell phone and flipped the flap. There was no network. It was working in the restaurant. She thought of dialling David from the landline and then registered the wind building up. Martha knew that anytime soon she would have to go inside the house. Anyhow, she did not dread being inside Barcaldine, she just needed some more time to understand everything before returning to the walls that had witnessed some really dreadful events.

She silently followed the colours of the exterior walls selected by Susan. A short smile appeared. She gazed at the prints of blue colour left by Ben's clumsy hands which they decided to leave as it is. A small playhouse stood near the periphery of the garden and Susan's favourite chair hung on a tree branch. The house was theirs after all, a consistent assurance resurfaced noticing all the little memories they had built so far.

***

Amie began on the same path towards Barcaldine after Martha left. The whole hike would cost her returning home late, but she had to make sure Martha had reached safely. She felt responsible for Martha. Barcaldine after all wasn't very far now. She followed the same route without Martha's knowledge. She must have reached by now, Amie thought, yet her concern couldn't rest until she was sure. After a shift of a few minutes, Amie reached the Barcaldine too.

Amie was yet to appear out of the glade when she spotted Martha sitting on the bench and staring at the house like a possessed woman. Amie panicked a bit and geared her feet, but instantly cut her long step short when Martha moved and lowered her head and squeezed her eyes. She felt assured when Martha got up and headed towards the house. Amie stood hidden behind the trees of Barcaldine. The wind had grown stronger and the sky was almost dusky now. Soon the only light reaching them would be a faint purple of the twilight.

Amie, feeling assured, stepped back, and turned to make her way out of Barcaldine's territory.

CHAPTER NINETEEN

Martha unlocked the door; the way she always did, but today nobody waited for her inside. The house was calm like any other inanimate object, nothing had changed about it, yet she felt as if she had returned to it after a brief stay away from it. It did not feel the same anymore.

The yellow light claiming the hallway drew a familiar feeling. She glanced around in search of something. At least it appeared so. But it was nothing more than a tender recognition of her belongings. She sat on her couch. The cold was being replaced by the warmth of the house. Martha tried to appear strong, showing opposition to whatever dishonoured the house, but she realized that her enemy wasn't around, she was just trying to fight her own mind; no one else except her was skeptical about Barcaldine's character, except Edward, but did his opinion matter? He had every reason to be biased.

It was bizarre but she decided to sleep on the couch in the living room. She didn't want to admit but she felt safer by being closer to the exit of the house. To feel calmer, she lit a small lamp beside the couch that gave off a very faint glow. The small circle of light felt assuring, as if it were a shield. She did not want to unrest her mind, wary of threats in the dark. She also switched off the warmer and instead used the chimney that David had refilled with unused wood. The crackling sound of the fire was an assuring company. Martha wanted some distraction; she picked up a book. It did help. Gradually, she picked up on the plot along the third page.

A distraction was caused when she heard the chandelier in the main hall move. The wind was strong, and old houses have a strange way of offering entry to relentless winds even when all the doors and windows are tightly shut. Martha tried not to bother much; she could not hold back the winds. She stayed in the welcoming lap of the couch and went on to read further. Soon she dozed off when her eyes felt heavy.

***

With that blasting noise, she opened her eyes so brusquely as if she hadn't slept at all. She felt a part of her mind was conscious all the way, watching over the house like a covert being, but a moment came when she fell into deep sleep. But now she was up. The wood in the chimney had reduced to cold grey ashes, which told her that she had slept for a while. There was no other sound to follow, for a moment Martha doubted herself, had she dreamt it? She looked around for any other signs. Nothing seemed to have broken. Everything was in its place. She scared herself, that was all. Martha again went inside the quilt and collapsed back into the void of the couch.

When the sound reappeared after a few minutes, this time she was clear that it wasn't a dream because it continued to grow even after her eyes were wide open. Martha rose with a gasp on her lips. Startled, she again searched around. It was not coming from a nearby room. But she recognized what it was. A door was beating against its frame. And the repetition was so consistent and controlled that it undoubtedly looked like the work of a living hand. It wasn't a very comforting deduction. She scolded herself; she had to stop this unnerving internal dialogue. With that Martha grabbed a torch and moved against the cold passage of air. Nothing stopped her from unlocking the main door; she went out, across the front porch, and stood before the house.

Surprisingly, the noise was much more audible now, as if coming from just above her head, which it was. She looked above her and saw it. The window, the same human sized opening of her room was hitting against its frame under an uncontrolled force of the winds. It pushed the window in and out like a leaf fluttering under a deadly storm. There was a sigh of rest but not relief. There was enough moonlight to conclude that it was just the wind doing it and not anything else. She cut her thoughts sternly.

Martha came back inside. The rest of the house was cold and dark. She wore her woollen robe and switched on the torch. The light beamed over the steps of the staircase rising up. Her moving feet were as silent as of an intruder, as if cautiously drawn to prevent from waking up an ambiguous entity. The hallway on the first floor was lit and its indirect reflection was peeping over the staircase. It inspired some confidence in Martha.

Her room was the first door on the left. The fluttering of the window continued heavily. It was just a few steps away now from being shut, thus putting an end to the sleeplessness of the night. Martha opened the door of her room. It was dark inside except the carpet of shadows laid by the soothing moonlight. Only one shadow was at unrest and Martha pointed the torch at it. The window was still fluttering but not as before, only slower now. She reached for the switch to light the room, but it did not work. She knocked the switch a couple of times but nothing happened. Seemed like another fault in the electrical lines. It made her sigh in irritation. With that Martha beamed the torchlight back at the window, and that was the moment when the course of the night changed.

The oval of the torch light now captured a face, which wasn't there before and which probably manifested only seconds ago out of the gushing wind. For a moment it seemed that the turbulent winds along with the play of moonlight drew a false apparition, but no, it was real, as real as her. A short but dense cry came out of her. Only hours ago what she was dreading stood now before her with no scope of doubt.

The man she saw stood frozen like a dummy with no suggestion of life in him; those eyes were just staring at her coldly, they were emotionless, no hint of sadness or hostility either. It was the clothes that made her realize it was a man. The old-fashioned suit shone with a pale white glint, while the pants disappeared beyond the knee into the darkness below. It looked as if the man had no feet and the white shirt was all smoke and ashes. Martha began to shiver that made the torch light flutter on that ghastly face. A part of the same light went right through the ghost. Martha felt as if somebody snatched the breath out of her lungs and locked her jaw to make her witness the horror silently without causing any interruption.

Suddenly, an abrupt change took over when the apparition swung its false body towards the window and away from Martha. Next came the terrifying. The man perched himself on the sill of the window. Martha blinked her eyes twice and before she could register it, the man jumped out into the thick cold air. How or why? There was no answer to it. She only heard his hoarse cry return to her muddled with the whistling of the winds. There was pain in that echo. It was unbearably noisy. Martha pressed her ears and screamed in fear.

She ran out of the room and down the stairs in a maddening cry. She could not even monitor the movement of her footsteps. She kept falling. Her legs were shaking. She imagined the man approaching her from behind and grabbing her by her shoulders. She rushed across the hallway to escape and was almost at the exit door when the next shock of the night knocked her. It happened when her face bumped into something and she fell heavily on the floor. The torch fell too, rolling on the floor beside her. It rolled until it stilled, the second time, to the thing she collided with, which were a pair of feet floating in air.

Martha began to shriek involuntarily when above that lifeless pair of feet; she saw a body, a woman hanging from the ceiling with life sucked by the rope tied around her neck. The room filled with the echoes of Martha's frantic screams when the body began to oscillate like a pendulum in the dim light of the hall. Her face turned so ugly with fear that it must have looked unrecognizable even to her. Martha got on her feet somehow and darted towards the door. She did not stop to look behind her when the rope twisted around the woman's neck and the body fell on the wooden floor like dead rotten meat. It was a nightmare; a grave encounter. Martha felt weak, her energy was draining out, her legs staggered but she continued for her safety.

Finally, the doorknob clicked and she came out falling on the front porch. Martha felt drained and weak. Her knees dragged her torso until she helplessly hit the open grass. Her chest was expanding and contracting as if it would burst out any second. Her eyes felt heavy and Martha realized she was on the verge of collapsing.

Before her eyes went black, the house growled, and she heard cries of brutal assaults inflicted on poor souls of a distant forgotten time. It felt as if a hundred souls were confessing their pain to her, all at once. Her body contorted like that of a hurt animal. But before another frightening event could take place, she fell into a deep unconscious sleep.

CHAPTER TWENTY

I

Edward was due to leave the town three days ago, but he chose against it. Something stopped him and he knew what it was. His next research was due. His sponsors were ready for him and his team was not amused with the delay. He was a crucial resource for his team after all. Not only was he the guiding hand but also the psychic tool of the group. The team relied on his sensory perceptions during their expeditions of everything that was considered demonic and unholy. Many a times, his abilities had saved them from unforeseen harm. He interacted with the spirits psychically while the team stood patiently, waiting for his instructions. He knew his team would be handicapped without him, but here, in Lanthom Cove, were emergencies.

Therefore, he posted his team to delay everything for a few weeks. After all, in a way, Barcaldine was a project too, a more personal one this time. Saving lives was one of the major reasons why he chose to practice paranormal research. That tragedy in his early years damaged most of his youth. There was no space left for any other fear to feast on his soul. His experiences made him efficiently committed to his work. Barcaldine's wrath also unleashed his psychic abilities. He did not know what triggered it, but others called it a gift. He wasn't thankful for it though, how could he be, after all he paid a huge price for it.

Since the past one week he lived the same routine. He would get up at eight and drink his coffee beside the window overlooking the hill. This was meditative for him. Donna served his breakfast by nine-thirty, however, this time the routine followed with exceptions. He would eat silently and obediently, never touch the newspaper nor ask for another serving. Donna could sense the change, but her professional training stopped her from interfering in the personal lives of their employers.

Edward strolled around eleven in the beautifully landscaped garden of his residency, almost half the size of the house. It was a dim sky. Wild vegetation had occupied a part of the site and Edward wished to keep it all untouched. These impressions of wilderness were sources of contemplation for him. Edward had asked for a bench to be placed in the midst of overgrown grass. He even refused to clear the path of golden dry leaves lying at the foot of the bench; he liked the ruffling noise it made when one stepped on it.

Edward sat on the bench facing a small iron gate, strapped with metal chains. The iron bars had also rusted beneath the heavy lock that barred its access. The moment he saw the car entering his driveway, he also recognized the person sitting behind the driver. He grew excited as if someone injected a shot of adrenaline into him. He instantly stood up and hurried towards the exit. He was out there to receive them even before the engines halted. The person inside the car saw him.

Martha got out of the car slowly. She looked tired and defeated. Her eyes displayed sadness and numbness in equal measure. Something was not right. Edward's heart began to beat faster. Had Barcaldine claimed its new victim?

Once she was out, she stood right there where the car left her with the same numbness. Edward wanted to receive her but he sensed she needed time. He was yet to know for what.

Her hands were cupped inside her long coat. She observed the sky for a few seconds and then looked around as if she was alone. Her behaviour had a nonchalant quality to it. She came here for a reason and Edward knew the reason was not a mild one.

Martha was cold even in the long coat protecting her. When the sun was up, she found herself lying on the grass. When she regained her senses, she felt changed. She was no more the same woman trying to fight the truth, but merely a powerless human, betrayed by her own convictions, trying to protect the boundaries of her world from otherwise tearing apart. But her convictions faltered last night. Barcaldine's past had been retold, and by no one else but the house itself. The game of hide and seek was over. There was nothing else to ignore, nothing more to believe, her house in truth, was haunted.

That is why Martha went inside the house. She had understood that Barcaldine's motive was not to take her life, but something else beyond her understanding. Unlike the others who were also played by the house, she was the only one who saw the light of the next day. She tried calling David; but couldn't reach him. She knew what she had to tell him; she would just ask him to come back. Martha changed her lowers and grabbed a long coat. A few blocks away was the cabstand. She knew her next destination and what she had to confess once she got there. Now, as she stood before him, she was at a loss of words, the entire gamut of events had left a dent.

Her hair fell to her sides like a loose scarf hung around her face. She headed towards Edward and reached him. What Martha then spoke was a pronouncement rather than what it should have been; an urgency for help. It could have also been the closure of all the apologies that she owed to him, for her ignorance towards his warnings. The words wrapped everything that was due.

"I saw it, Mr. Woods. I suffered my personal tragedy."

II

When she told him about the Willards, Edward felt betrayed. A past that was his right to be aware of, life kept it from him until now. It was a painful revelation for a victim and ignorance on his part as a paranormal researcher. There were times when he considered going back to Lanthom Cove and getting the necessary permissions from the owner of the house – surely there would be one – and attempt to unravel the mystery. But he chose rather against it. He had exposed himself to various sites that were marked haunted, but he still did not feel enough courage to face Barcaldine. He didn't even want the tabloids to know anything about his history with the house.

Back then nobody ever got to know where the third boy vanished after the deaths of the other two kids. But Edward only returned after a gap of two decades, bought a residency away from Barcaldine, far from the main Cove Hill. No one could deduce that this man was the same boy who vanished decades ago. He came back with a new identity and a new life.

Barcaldine was the only hell for him in the whole wide world, and Edward had been preparing himself for this unfinished business. He knew a day would come when he will be compelled to do justice to the deaths of his friends, who didn't deserve to die the way they did.

Martha refused to talk in the library, so Edward chose the safety of a cozy reading room on the ground floor. She further discouraged the idea of lifting the drapes up; the dusky light outside stirred dark shadows in her head. The artificial yellow light seemed warmer and suitable. This time the coffee did not stale either, she drank it while the aroma was still fresh and strong. Martha wrapped herself with a warm drape delivered by Donna. She collected herself on the couch like a rescued survivor who demanded care.

"The story of the Willards makes sense! An entire family met its demise after the unfortunate loss of another member. And the woman, you said she went crazy, could this be the reason behind that inflicted madness on Paul and his insane ending?" said Edward.

But he wasn't really talking to Martha while he attempted to stitch the two events.

"The man jumped from the window; Wesley was found lying on the porch. Was the history being repeated through us on that horrible night?"

He retrieved from his analysis and looked at Martha as he further went deeper into decoding the events.

"Spirits at times get stuck in time loops. They become bound to repeat the same events that left a dent in them at the time of death. But rarely does it happen that they choose mortals to re-enact those events. They do not have that kind of command and power over time and space, to be able to bring a different entity into their cursed play. They are like puppets stuck in an act. They do not have control."

Edward treaded hastily behind the couch. His hands were clenched at his back trying to hold an outburst of uncontrollable rush of thoughts. The minute he shaped his next interpretation; he could not keep his excitement.

"...or, have they become vengeful? Yes! This could be it. They blame the world for what happened with them."

"But they didn't kill me, even when they had the chance to do so. They spared me, why?" Martha indicated the lack of consistency in his deduction.

He hurriedly sat next to her. His mind was running like a power house.

"Martha, evil spirits thrive on fear and pain; they don't need a reason to assault someone. Sometimes death changes a soul. It can turn evil even if it wasn't before. Maybe they have weakened with time. Their last interaction with a living soul happened thirty years ago. They certainly did frighten you and fear in humans fuels their power."

"It all sounds so ominous, can something so unknown run so rationally?

"Indeed, it can. This is what our study is all about. A strong mind does not give in easily; it is a barrier against spirits. Paul, Wesley, and I; all three of us were drunk. You might find it strange, but alcohol brings down that barrier, makes us much more vulnerable. I believe that's what must have made it easier for Barcaldine to infiltrate and possess. The human perception needs to broaden up. Before science proved, oxygen was unknown. But wasn't it still a fact? It was. The discovery only made us aware of it."

"What you say makes sense. But I still feel that there is more to what happened with me last night. They didn't even touch me, if they have become enough capable of manifesting at will, then they could have easily attacked. But the spirits only revealed to me what marked their end. This has to have a meaning behind it."

After she had expressed herself, Martha realized the fact hidden in her words; her house was hosting more than one spirit, out of which she had encountered two and the rest two were still dormant; for lack of a better word. She felt another stroke of shiver, but none comparable to what hit her last night. She now bore the strength to surpass this one.

"You are not wrong in saying that," Edward said.

"How much time do we have before they are at their strongest?" Martha questioned.

"Nobody can assess that. Spirit world is full of mysteries. It's been around three months since you moved here. They never suggested their presence to you until now. They are enough powerful now to reveal themselves, and that I am sure of. Have you ever had any nightmares before in this house?

"How do you know?"

"That means you did."

"Yes. We had just moved. I saw myself getting down in the basement and there I saw a girl sitting against the wall. She was crying, there was a foul smell in the air and the gore off her throat; I remember all of it. Her body was bruised from everywhere, and her throat was slit." Martha shrunk her eyes; she did not want to declare the next statement but she did. "I think she was one of the Willard's children, that Mrs. Willard murdered."

And that added another count to the ghosts that had revealed themselves. How frightening would be the fourth one? Martha thought

"How can a mother do that to her own child...?" Edward said.

"I can't imagine it either. But that woman did. She might have cut her by the throat," Martha said feeling painfully disgusted.

"Hmm. Spirits find it easier to channel through dreams, especially when they are weak. May be that is what happened with you."

"But why only me? None of my kids or my husband ever mentioned seeing anything. Why it's just me? Why they chose me? It's insane!"

"Yes, it is insane, but may be something about you makes it easy for them to connect with you and only you. Yes, it might seem absurd, but this is how it works."

Her eyes were still. Comprehension of so much being told was a task beyond her knowledge. What was happening? All the explanations seemed to confuse an already complicated reasoning.

"Mr. Woods, I don't know how to respond to what all you have told me," Martha began with regret, "My world has become unstable and beyond what I can handle. All I want is them out of my house, before they hurt my family. I might look weak, but I am a strong woman. My husband isn't in town, my kids are away but still I made a decision, because I saw it with my own eyes and I don't want anyone else's approval anymore to validate what I witnessed. I also know that these spirits want something. This might just be a feeling without any rational foundation but I know they also want to be out and free from the prison of Barcaldine. I just need to know what they want from me."

"Martha, I hope you realize what you are asking for. You want to communicate with the spirits? Is that what you want? You have no idea what it means. It might lead to unexpected conclusions. It is a very dangerous task," David was stern this time.

Martha detached herself from his warning.

"I know, Mr. Woods. It is an extremely dangerous task for a woman like me," she paused and then added, "but only without your help..."

Edward understood what the women had asked for. Had the moment to pay his destined due arrived? He had been foreseeing it since the time he met Martha at the party. He knew that every consecutive meeting with Martha was also pushing him closer to it. *Time has come*; he told himself. Agreeing to help her meant facing Barcaldine again, being inside that house and welcoming all those memories that he had managed to suppress deep within.

When Martha turned to face him again, his expressions lightened, and she knew her demand had secured the winning position.

"Would you, Mr. Woods?" She said again.

Edward finally marked the beginning of a great chase with a simple nod in approval.

CHAPTER TWENTY-ONE

A thin white fog had settled by the time they decided to leave. Edward demanded to meet Amie, who he assumed could assist with more information about the history of the Willards. Before leaving his house, he went to his room upstairs and on his return carried a box that looked like a small chest box. He didn't tell Martha what it was, even though he saw the question and curiosity in her eyes.

They settled in the front seats of his car and left. The rain had come down to a silent drizzle, leaving tiny spots of water on the windows. Martha unwrapped herself from the shelter of the drape, the car was warm from inside. Edward was clearly a slow driver. In truth it was intentional, to buy more time to build strength, to be able to stand rigid before the fight ahead. He didn't know what role was he playing now? Was he a professional who aided people with his abilities or was he the victim who was going back to seek revenge?

"I suppose you haven't told your husband yet," Edward said while his eyes and hands were carefully following the route.

"I tried calling him, but could not reach him."

She discreetly lifted her fingers covering her mobile screen and glimpsed at the signals. Two bars had recovered.

"Do you intend to tell him?" he paused and then added, "Afterall this can't stay hidden."

Martha had been asking the same question to herself since morning. The question pondered while she was on her way to the wood's residency.

"He would get to know. He returns in a day. In the morning, I wanted to call him right away, but now I want to wait. I want to confront Barcaldine with you, and even if I manage to reach him now, he will not believe me. He might even blame you. I might become fearful again. Moreover, he has hidden things from me in the past, and if he was also aware about the Willards before we moved here, I fear this might leave a dent in our relationship. What I saw last night, I can now imagine the horror you went through..." she said turning to him.

She waited before going further.

"I know I need help, and only you can help me. I also know my husband, and that his reluctance will only make the task harder. My kids are my biggest concern; I do not want them to step into this hell after they return hoping for a safe haven. My family is away right now and in some uncertain way, I feel relieved. There is no other place my family can go to; neither would I want to sell this inferno to someone else. There is a lot at stake and this is the best I can do right now. Even though I know it can change me as a person for the rest of my life, if anything goes wrong."

Edward was struck by her words. Martha understood her situation and options transparently. Edward was relieved to see that she was strong and stable, even after escaping the frightening night. People usually are incapable of keeping their sanity alone; forget about intelligence and clear talk. This woman processed both in her difficult times.

The car was half way through and reached the Cove Hill. The view from the steep lane made the sky look even closer, and when the lightening thundered, it felt even the skies could resonate with the anguish of the lost spirits of Barcaldine.

The road was wrecked by frequent tearing from rainwater. It made the car shiver to its sides like a rickety bus. For a moment, along a tricky curve, Martha panicked fearing that the car would topple over the cliff. But Edward balanced the wheel in time. At a junction, the road diverged into two lanes, one ran around the peripheries of the hill; the one she knew. The other went through a deep shadowy forest. The one that went into the forest was quite narrow and could jam two cars easily if they tried to pass each other, and yet Edward took this one.

The dense trees crowding from both sides were thick and tall like long walls of a maze. The headlights glowed brightly to their full strength and yet looked weak before the pitch darkness of the forest. Everything was alarmingly silent too. The creatures in the woods might be peeping at the passing car, keeping a constant eye on the intruders, and that made Martha feel an indescribable threat. It felt worse than worrying about falling from the cliff. Even the lightening from the sky was not visible anymore. After an alert driving of twenty minutes, the unknown track again met with the periphery of the hill and once again brought them back to the terrain where humans lived.

After half a mile more, the car reached the end of the hill. From here the plains took over. The church and the cemetery came into view, racing the blood into their veins. When the car was close enough to catch the biblical facade, they both exchanged a look of silent recognition of a mutual memory. The car accelerated and the church was left behind on its throne with greater speed.

It was seven in the evening when the car stopped on the rutted path from where Amie's house was close. Martha knew the address; Amie had told where she lived when they first met. It was simple and recalling it wasn't hard. The car could not go beyond the large pool of water. The house was only a few meters away now. Martha had to walk till the door carrying a wide umbrella that could shade two people easily. It had not been even twenty-four hours since she last met Amie, still so much had happened.

Martha saw two women walking out of Amie's house. She realized Amie must be seeing off her guests so she quickened her steps to reach Amie before she closed the door. Martha almost slipped on the muddy path and closely tip-toed the rest of the way. When she reached the door, she could only see Amie's hand up to her elbow shutting it down.

"Amie!" she called for her.

The door was quickly opened at the call, but there was someone else standing at the door. The woman was not Amie.

"Oh, I am sorry, I thought you were Amie. Is she at home?"

The woman studied Martha for several seconds in an odd manner. Martha was shivering in the cold and she had already begun yearning for the warmth of the car and wished that the woman could be quicker in replying.

"No, Amie is not at home."

When the woman answered, Martha sighed in a noticeable petulant manner.

"When is she expected to be back? Would you please let her know that Martha came to see her?"

The woman looked at Martha again, a weird silence grew between them. Martha was a bit aggressive in her tone but it wasn't the best time to be patient.

"Will you please, Miss?" Martha said desperately.

"I think you are not aware," the woman said.

"Aware of what?"

"Amie is missing."

Martha's impatient face dropped stunned on the answer.

"She never returned home since she left in the afternoon yesterday," the woman added.

CHAPTER TWENTY-TWO

The car headed towards its mission after the setback.

"This is insane, I just met her yesterday. I left her on that path. Did something happen to her? Did someone harm her?

"That sounds unlikely. These things don't really happen here," Edward said casually.

Edward felt a bit ashamed of himself. More than the fact that the woman was missing, the help they had missed out on bothered him. The rain was literally pouring now. One could not see anything from the windshield and the wipers did their best to fight the rain away.

"The weather is quite bad. It doesn't go this far that often," Edward said. Martha had to be distracted. He knew she couldn't afford to unrest her mind by worrying about Amie.

"What the fuck is happening!! Why is everything becoming so complicated?" Martha cried out loudly and unexpectedly

Her frustrated tone was a surprise even to her. Edward could not distract his eyes from the track, knowing that the mysterious weather could have its way any second. With his spare hand, he patted her shoulder reassuringly. Martha sighed towards the window; she couldn't afford to lose her calm, not right now, when she needed every ounce of her attention to deal with Barcaldine.

"Martha, a lot lies ahead of us. Her disappearance will be dealt; there are people to take care of it. You have emergencies to deal with. Do not lose your strength; you will need a lot of it."

She inhaled deeply against her frustration.

"Yes, you are right," she said.

Martha realized that she was no more guiding the route back to Barcaldine, yet Edward was taking all the right turns.

"Martha, before we enter the house, there are things I need to tell you. You need to fully understand the nature of the entities we will be invoking." He began, "Human nature is predictable to us, and even though these spirits have been through the human world and largely recognize with the same mindset; yet they are not the same anymore. The restrictions that bind us to the limitations of a mortal body are no longer applicable to them."

Edward suddenly thumped on the brakes and the car came to a sudden arrest. A thick log of tree had fallen on the road. The road was blocked. Water had clogged around the fallen dead trunk and suggested that it had been lying there for a while now. They checked the stretch, not a single car was visible in the approachable distance. Nobody must have passed after the tree was razed off by its roots.

Edward reversed the gear, the car lights wavered, and the tires took a backward roll. There was another road that opened to her house.

"Let's take the other route. I know where to navigate." Edward announced.

The back ride caused another half an hour delay. In addition, was the limited visibility due to the emerging fog.

"You were explaining something, Mr. Woods." Martha wanted him to continue before her mind began to wander again.

"Yes," he cleared his throat. "What I am trying to differentiate here is simple, yet a reason for worry. For example, when we get angry, we have two choices; we either suppress it or choose to vent out our frustration, right? Similarly, if someone else feels anger towards us, they have the same choices. If a person chooses to release their anger, the most he or she can do is attack, a physical assault that we can seize within our possible strength. There is a simple difference in here. First, you can never know if you have infuriated these entities, neither can you predict their assault at any point nor defend yourself completely against it. If you can't see something, how can you predict their actions? It is that simple. They might be playing with you and you would never even know. You have to be very alert about every second spent communicating with them. Your intuition can be helpful though."

Edward stressed on some particular words outlining the seriousness of the subject. The effort was to make Martha understand what she had chosen.

"You might feel a burst of unrecognizable emotions. They might make you see what happened with them. This can make you feel for them too. However, they do not want your pity, they are just seeking strength, which they can get if they manage to weaken the barrier between them and us. We must remember, if we open a door to their world, we must do it with a shield, and this shield is nothing but your lack of emotions for them. The best you can do is acknowledge their story but don't empathize with them. Do you understand?"

Martha nodded in agreement, even if she only understand it on the periphery. It was a complex game, this much she was sure of by now, and she had to follow the rules, she had to follow everything Edward had to offer.

The car was parked right in front of the iron gate of the mansion. The iron bars cast clear shadows on the ground under the glow of lamp poles whose light flickered under the rain. Inside the Barcaldine territory, a narrow lane ran in the midst of the grass from the gate up to the dark house. The lane was barely visible now. Martha glanced at the screen of her phone several times hoping for David's name to appear any second even though she had decided against calling him.

Edward bent over the rear seat and got hold of the box he had collected before leaving. Martha recognized it. A curious look resurfaced while Edward thumbed the lock and its cubical lid opened. It was a beautifully ornamented box and bore inscriptions and patterns taken from various ancient art styles and that too from a variety of eras. The Chinese art honoured a separate large space at the top of the lid with an artwork representing a woman in kimono. Around her was wrapped a Chinese dragon chaining her from head to toe. Martha found the Chinese depiction quite beautifully carved out.

Edward took out a small electronic gadget that was a palm-long in length. Martha expected more distinct items belonging to some ancient era and suitable to be found inside this equally bizarre box. Next came a small voice recorder supported with an attached microphone. Edward went through the stuff revising his checklist and Martha waited patiently beside him. Edward then lifted a wooden bracket. Below the bracket, the lower section was spaciously designed to fit extra stuff.

"We will need all these things. These tools will help us in detecting the presence of any spirit in and around the place," he said indicating the need for the electronic equipment.

Placing the wooden bracket on his lap, he lifted a small envelope made of rich cloth and its protruding skin suggested some solid objects inside it. Clasping the fabric between his palms, he drew a serious glance.

"These we need to protect ourselves," he said.

He opened the flap and introduced a small object out of it. By the tiny hook at the top, Martha recognized it was a pendant of some kind, but not an ordinary one. When she strained to identify it, she realized that it depicted an enormous eye coloured with shades of black and royal blue.

"It's an eye..." she said

"Yes, it's the Eye of Horus," he said steadily.

Martha didn't understand the term. She didn't have to convey it. Hardly anyone must be aware of what it was.

"Eye of Horus is an ancient Egyptian symbol. It is a very powerful symbol of protection and strength. If looked closely, this eye can be differentiated into various odd and even geometrical shapes, each having its own significance. It is believed to have great healing and protection power against the evil. It stands for the power of wisdom and truth and is famous in many occult practices. But theory is not everything, it is nothing without faith, and I have faith in it. I have had my experiences with its power."

Martha wanted to believe in it like him. But instead, she had faith in Edward, and somehow, she knew that was enough for now. Next in line were more expected objects. There was a Christian cross and the most ancient one in design; the Greek cross. This one was ornamented with complex designs on the arms, equal in length, and unlike the common Latin cross. There was a pair of two inside an equally immaculate piece of cloth.

Martha looked a little surprised and Edward saw it.

"You have a question in your eyes. What is it?"

Martha took a moment before she spoke.

"I never knew you believed in religious symbols; it is quite unlike for a scientific man like you," said Martha.

"To the logic of personal belief; I am not very religious, I admit. However, I believe more in their significance."

"What does that mean?"

"The spirits of Barcaldine would have been Christians when they were alive, and theirs was an era of community and common faith. It somehow bonded people, unlike the world today."

"Yes, but how is it related?"

Edward drew a sensible look towards her. She was asking right and worthy questions.

"In every way. Their belief is what marks its significance for us. The cross is a symbol of faith in the lord for every Christian. People die, but their belief goes on with them in spirit. We will be using their beliefs against them, because even though they are dead, their belief is not. Now the same cross after death is a symbol of fear for them. It continues to represent the most powerful and has the same effect on their mind. Thus, this cross becomes our tool of protection."

"And what about our faith, doesn't that count?" Martha asked.

"Of course it does, your faith will only magnify its protection over you. Your faith in the cross, and here I mean strong faith, will incredibly strengthen its power. Because now it is not just their fear that works in your favour, but also your own faith that weaves protection for you. Remember, it is all a game of faith and mind. That is why I said earlier?"

Martha tried to recall all of his previous statements, which indeed had increased in count uncontrollably so far. All his theories seemed to relate in some or the other way. Edward continued speaking when he realized Martha was unable to recall the one he demanded.

"The only way to protect yourself is by keeping your sanity," he said.

This time Martha could understand it, unlike the moment when it was first told in the library. The facts were clearly crafting the desired outcome. She almost felt like a student being taught about subjects she never enrolled for. It seemed like a grand preparation for a battle. The situation was quite literally the same, except that in this case, the attack would not spill blood on both sides.

Edward filled the empty space of the hook with a rugged thread. The thread came out from the mouth of the hook to sufficiently tie around a neck as fragile as that of Martha's. He released the Eye of Horus to his left pocket. There were a few more articles in the lower mysterious section of the box but Edward did not progress towards them. They were left unmoved before the covering tray resurfaced and drowned them back into the darkness.

Martha dropped her feet on the grey road. The green grass was seeping out from below the iron gate. Edward fixed his stare on the house and felt a shiver over his skin.

Martha pushed the gate in. The resonance of its movement around the hinges flashed a few images from the night of 1976. Edward could somewhat again see Wesley standing before the chained gate, stubbornly beating the irons with his fist, and Paul jumping over his feet trying to go over the wall to get in. He hadn't acknowledged it yet, but he was aware of the possibility of reencountering his beloved friend.

He wondered what the house must have altered in Wesley, if he still was trapped inside. Was he now one with the darkness of Barcaldine like the others or was he still the victim of that night waiting for his release? Edward knew he would know soon.

Edward followed Martha on the raw path with no grass to hold its exposed mud. He walked rather slowly. She did not turn to check on him knowing the reason behind his delayed steps. Edward located the window; it was still there, the one that served as the entrance to the doom that awaited them. The sight of it stung him and he quickly sighed away. He rushed his steps leaving footprints that instantly vanished in a matter of seconds and joined Martha.

CHAPTER TWENTY-THREE

I

The inside of the house was calm but observant, Edward assimilated. It just took him one step inside Barcaldine to verify the presence of those entities. His mind marked them as *distributed*, referring to their vigilance all around the house. The place was enveloped by a dark energy, not a corner was left untouched. His psychic sensitivity was active to its full potential. He looked at Martha with a mix of emotions; respect, pity, sympathy; she had endured like a martyr. Before they sat around the centre table in the grand room, Martha left the door unlocked; just in case!

The grand room was mellow and less affected somehow, relatively adaptable than the rest of the Barcaldine. It was the part of the house that was occasionally used and stood as the largest space on the ground floor, almost thrice the length and twice the width of the living room and required the custody of at least three big chandeliers to illuminate every inch of it. Martha stood near a window never used even till today. She stood there preoccupied while Edward emptied his box. Martha was wearing a cross around her neck, so was Edward, and in addition to it was his Eye of Horus supporting them.

He inserted a cassette into the small mini-recorder and placed it on the table. The next thing was an EMF meter which he explained could indicate the closeness of these spirits by reading the energy changes in the room. When he switched it on, the needle immediately jumped and settled to a reading few digits above zero. Edward was startled at first but realized that it was expected out of Barcaldine.

When he advanced around the drawing room to investigate further, the numbers gave a consistent reading everywhere without much fluctuation except at certain corners. This consistent reading indicated that the supernatural presence was largely uniform everywhere. He was right about the house being enveloped with it. It was indeed watchful.

"It can sense every move," murmured Edward.

"Who?" Martha whispered.

"Personality is yet unknown, but it has its smell everywhere. It is aware of every corner. Be cautious, it can be one entity or a collective presence."

Martha clenched her fist around the cross. She left the company of the noisy window and ran back to sit beside Edward on the carpet.

"Don't be afraid. Remember what I have told you," He reassured her.

Martha nodded faintly. She was finding it hard to recollect all the theories he had shared with her so far. Even though it became challenging now, yet she strained to remember.

"Martha, listen to me carefully. What I am going to do now will seem frightening to you, but steel yourself. You can stand it, I know, and remember, I am here with you."

He looked straight at her as he continued, "I am going to make a contact with the spirits of Barcaldine. We need to know what they want, the reason of their unrest and anguish. You might see some changes in me as I am the medium, but do not panic. They cannot harm me. They will just be using my body and that too only if I allow them to and if they choose to. Do you understand?"

Martha nodded again in a child-like innocence. There was nothing left to do or say.

"At any point if you feel frightened, just close your eyes or recite any prayer that grants you strength. Divert your mind immediately, but just restrain yourself from reacting. I know it is easier said than done, but we don't have many options. My team is not here with me; you are my only support." He added lastly, "Have faith in me, and your god."

It sounded like the last words between two warriors who were about to enter a battle. Martha gulped down the fear and sat attentively to reassure Edward. With that, Edward switched on the record button that lit with a red blinking spot.

II

Edward sat silently for a few minutes, his eyes were closed and he began to mumble incoherent words. They were merely whispers to Martha's ears which made them sound strange and barbaric. When Edward started conjuring the spirits, there was a sudden change in the modulation of his voice. It was sharp, demanding, and louder than she had ever seen him use before. Strangely and unsettlingly, it reminded Martha of the beginnings of wizards casting spells.

"We are here, here for you, to ease your pain. Come and tell us what is that you want, why are you still in this house when you should have left long ago? I ask you to release yourself and share with us your pain without causing us any harm."

There was simply nothing. The room was silent as before. Not even a leaf moved, that could indicate or stand as a response to the call. No response was somewhat relieving to Martha, but then she reminded herself why they were here. A response was necessary; they could not delay it.

Edward waited for a few more minutes and started again.

"What is it that you want? Why are you here? If you do not wish to make a contact, then I command you to leave this house in the name of lord that is watching you, loves you, and asks you to return!"

The dead silence lingered like a shadow adding to the uncertainty of what was to come. Everything seemed to be stuck between possibilities, yet refusing to move to either of the sides. When each of his call went unheard, Edward raised his voice, and this time he wasn't kind, he was harsh like a storm.

"I said, make a contact or leave!!"

Suddenly, an abrupt rise in the reading of the meter was recorded. The numbers on the digital screen changed furiously. Edward realized someone was finally answering his call. He looked alarmingly at the EMF meter. The rise meant only one thing; an entity was heading towards them with frightening speed. He had never seen the needle rise so sharply before. His heart began to run faster and he suddenly screamed, "STOP". His bulging eyes were blood red, and his palm stood out rigidly in front of him like a shield. The instant his echo died, the reading on the meter became still, barring any further increase in the numbers.

It shook Martha. She opened her eyes that she had kept closed all along reciting prayers that she believed in. With this, she realized it had begun. She stared at him alarmed.

Her limp mouth could not bring words out of them. She began to breathe faster to meet her racing heart. The countdown had begun, and the only exit now would be the revelation of Barcaldine.

Edward evaluated the proximity of the entity, it was closer than ever, hovering somewhere near. Its residue was evident. His decision to cease its progress was timely realized. The presence of the spirit was clear, palpable, and very much strong, and it drew an instant conclusion; letting it use a mortal body would be lethal. I can't do that, he told himself.

His intuition was right though. He looked at his recorder whose light blinked rapidly while a sound was being captured. A spirit was making contact, but which one was it, Edward could not say.

"Why are you here? Tell us, who are you?" Edward demanded.

As if to obey his command, a distant echo hit them. It was hard to describe its origin and it sounded like uneven notes of an electronic flute, crushing the air with its force. It began with a suggestion at first and then suddenly roused to a scream. It was a terrible noise, one painful to ears. Edward's voice died under its intensity. Martha scrunched her eyes and barred her ears with both hands. It was unbearable. The noise echoed; every inch of glass present in the room, in any form, began to scuttle. Edward felt vibrations inside his chest. He wrapped his arms around his ribs fearing that the noise might damage his heart.

Then came a raucous blast from somewhere inside the house. It sounded like a sharp gunshot from a heavy tool. It was followed by a crisp rumble of dying cries and the house fell silent again. The whole encounter was quick but jarring, and its debris lingered for several minutes.

When they opened their eyes, they found the grand chandelier swaying softly in air. Martha crossed her arms around her knees and sunk her head inside her lap. She was left in shivers, but the whispers of her rapid breaths were now soothing after that deafening echo.

The meter reading trailed back to a sudden low. It meant the spirit had returned back to its corner in the house. However, the peace wasn't declared yet, the entities still shadowed Barcaldine.

"A very strong spirit made contact," Edward stated timidly.

Martha still had her head buried in her lap. Her fear had conquered the best of her. Her hands felt numb and legs unbalanced. The echoes lingered in her head like a throbbing pain. She heard a click and then Edward speaking again, but it wasn't him doing the talking this time, it was the mini recorder revisiting the past few minutes. She lifted her head and looked at him.

As recorded, first there was the initial call urging a contact. Then after a brief silence came a series of unknown voices. Surprisingly, and unlike the cacophony heard before, the device recorded discernible voices, human like but only distant and unclear. There were whispers, struggle for words, and suppressed cries, and within all that there was a message, delivered through a disturbed radio frequency. And the most shocking part; the voices belonged to children, and undoubtedly the children of the Willard family.

That credible portion of the tape left Martha in complete disbelief. She covered her mouth locking a cry. What they gathered was a disordered message but legible. Edward hurriedly grabbed a piece of paper and began to scribble down. He replayed the tape repeatedly to listen to it over and over again. His writing was so quick that there were hardly any breaks to ponder upon. After he finished, he gave a brief absorbing look to the paper, and showed what he had scribbled to Martha. She reluctantly moved and took it. It wasn't any bigger than the size of a receipt.

HeLP....uhsss...kill...d...(roar)..we ..thra..pd...fhather kill..d.....(whispers).she wouldn't let us go....not..(mute)...he..lp....mother..(mute).mhurder... bhass..(roar)...mehnt....gho away....

"Please read the words aloud," he demanded.

Martha scanned the paper, which looked more legible than the recording, and began to read slowly but firmly.

"Help... us... killed... we trapped," she stopped speaking, and looked at him fearfully for a second, and then continued, "Father killed... she would not let us go... Not... Help... mother, murder bass... ...meant... go.... Away."

The gaps in between indicated the lapses recorded in the tape. She looked at him bewildered. But Edward was occupied. The contact had been made successfully, but he realized that the assortment of words was only somewhat reconfirming what they already knew. This hadn't helped much. They desperately needed to discover another angle to the truth. The only exception was one message transmitted orderly in the muddled words; it dictated a valuable consideration. Edward narrowed his eyes towards the floor.

"These kids are trapped in here," Martha said in shock.

"Yes, and it suggests that their mother is holding them imprisoned here."

It was somewhat obvious, Mrs. Willard's continued devilish insanity. But Edward dared not to soak his mind bluntly in words, not at least when he was inside Barcaldine.

"Their cry for help... they were murdered by their own mother, and now they want to be free but can't. It's-It's terrible," Her voice began to break.

"Yes, but knowing this is not enough. It doesn't sort out the puzzle. Yes, the woman lost herself, and she probably must be in the same condition even after death. But then what about Mr. Willard? And you saw him too, isn't it?" Edward said.

"Yes, I did, but what about him?"

"Why is he here? What is holding him back?"

"Depression ate him, right?" Martha asked.

"Yes."

"So, can it be possible that..." she grew doubtful.

"Go on... Say what are you suggesting?" Edward persuaded her encouragingly.

"I don't know. It is all so confusing."

"Say what you are thinking, Martha," Edward said. He needed help to make his head work.

"Do you think he is responsible for the death of the others and is keeping everyone trapped in here? There has to be some strong motive behind his stay. After all, even he went insane. He may have refused to leave his family even after death," Martha finally established.

"Hmm, that is possible. But we cannot be sure of it. However, we can be sure that Mrs. Willard was behind her children's death. The voices clearly said in the recording, she will not let us go, which clearly means it is their mother and not their father."

"Yes, you're right." Martha said disappointedly. "If this is the truth, then we are back to square one, why is Mr. Willard still here?"

"I think there should be something more to this message, only if I can arrange them in a correct order." Edward said.

Martha examined the scrawl again. She read every word carefully, examining them. Suddenly, a stream of excitement resurfaced.

"Wait a minute, look at this!" she said promptly.

"What?"

"The words say, 'Father killed'...."

"Yeah... so?"

"Mr. Willard was not killed, he committed suicide. He died out of his own will. I don't know if I am carrying random deductions, but it does invite suspicion. And I am sure about him. Amie told me so and I saw it with my eyes too."

After she was finished, Edward realized that it did make sense. He hurriedly pulled her arm holding the paper towards him and   looked at the words.

"Father killed, it could have been father died or killed himself... I don't know... does it work that way?" Martha grew doubtful again.

"It can be true; it might not be. Though I know that spirits are very precise with their choice of words. The channel between the two worlds is already very weak and they are aware of that. They would want to avoid misunderstanding, especially when they are seeking help. This has been my experience. Their messages are always aimed to the point."

"Then we can consider this literally, is that right?"

He walked away from her. The recurring look of contemplation returned.

"And if this is true, if there is someone else behind his death, which is hard to imagine looking at the facts we know, then I suppose there is more to this story that no one knows about."

Edward's words were somewhat true. But what was the truth? The night had progressed for both the living and the dead. The rain continued and not a single person could be seen strolling on the streets. The town had slept, keeping their doors and windows locked tight, allowing the storm to pass, without letting it know about the life and the mystery that rested within this town.

Time was running. He knew as the night advanced, the world of the spirits only grew stronger. There was much to be gathered in very little time. He had planned to leave the house before midnight.

Edward sat undecidedly on the couch, indistinctively looking around the place in search of his next hook, a prospective push. It was helpful that the spirits had cooperated so far. But now the question was; if these spirits were trapped inside Barcaldine, how could he alleviate their misery?

All the equipment lay helpless on the centre table. The red eye of the recorder had settled too. The slightly wrinkled piece of paper lay on the table. Martha felt as if the eyes of the hidden spectators were all aimed at her. She switched on all the three chandeliers to feel more secure under the protection of light.

"What do we do now?" Martha asked breaking the silence. The extending silence was weakening her determination. She needed to talk, to know what was happening, and to get out of Barcaldine as soon as possible.

"I don't know. I think of another contact, but it isn't advisable to make contact with the unknown repeatedly. I have taken the most chance that is allowed at a time," Edward said firmly.

Martha did not find the uncertainty in his voice helpful. Even Edward, after stating his words, regretted having shown frailty. It wasn't about vanity, but he had to protect her faith in him. He couldn't lose that.

"But I know it is not impossible, it would not end in disappointment," he added quickly sounding determined. Martha soaked her tears in that had almost resurfaced.

"Martha, have you ever encountered temperature changes in and around your house? Like some rooms or corners feel strange for no apparent reason in comparison to the rest of the house."

Martha gave a reviewing thought. But couldn't come up with anything.

"No, nothing of that sort," she said after paying a serious thought.

"Are you sure?" Edward stressed again.

She nodded.

Edward felt a compelling tension around him, like something wanted to be revealed and concluded, but only if he could locate that seam which could guide him to the truth. He could swear they were very close to it. They were just skipping a deadly important detail.

"Hold on –" Martha spoke promptly.

Edward turned to her in anticipation.

"What – what happened?"

"Ben – my son, I remember! He did complain of a sudden rise and fall in the temperature of his room. We thought it was some fault with the heating system. But when we got it checked, it was working fine."

"Where is that room? Tell me," Edward questioned hoping that it to be that prospective push; the passage leading them to the truth.

"On the first floor." replied Martha gravely.

***

They quickly took the staircase and landed in the uninviting hallway. The bleak dullness was completely new for Martha. She had followed this hallway for months now but never felt it to be so detached to her. The distance to Ben's room was a short walk from the landing. Vast sizes of isolated weary houses stood with distaste in this situation.

The door to Ben's room finally appeared. Martha had checked her cell phone five times during the period of an hour, just hoping one lucky call from David. For some reason, now she really wanted to hear from him. Have him beside her. She also thought of dialling him but now wasn't the time. She tugged the phone inside her tight jeans making it inaccessible to her hasty hands. On the other side, Edward curiously scanned the screen of his trustworthy meter, vigilant of any moment suggesting an uncalled attack.

The door to Ben's room was already open. Purple light filtered through the windows and left blue patches all over. Unlike the mellow feel of that shade, the room was freezing. Edward felt prickles over his skin. The readings on the meter adjusted to this change. Edward remarked the energy to be evident but not furious in nature. It was somewhat frightening yet relieving to Martha. Frightening because she had unknowingly left her son exposed to a supernatural entity, but fortunately it was not vengeful.

The chill inside the room could have been the result of that one open window if it wasn't so unnaturally cold. It made Martha shiver under her heavy coat. She had never felt anything like this before and it made her pity Ben, who wasn't lying.

"Lots of cold spots, too many in fact." Edward puffed out a breath of cold air from his mouth.

"Are they of any harm?" Martha asked worrying about any prolonged damage on Ben.

"No; like I said, this entity isn't furious. The most this one can do is make its presence felt evidently. At least, I do not feel an air of rage coming from it."

At least was not good. At this stage she feared anything less than certain.

Martha had the possession of the scribbled paper and the voice recorder. Edward kept it switched on, there was still a possibility of sounds getting recorded, carrying disguised messages.

"This entity is always moving; it is never still, but stays only to this room. I can feel it wandering around us."

Martha felt as if a sharp perilous spear was hung around them with the opportunity of stabbing them at will, from anywhere it wished.

"We know you are here, who are you? Do you have anything to tell us?" Edward called.

Martha stared at Edward. Was it another attempt of a contact? No, it was different; he did not mumble those strange words like earlier.

"Come on, come on, do something. What is this whole mystery about?" Edward murmured impatiently as he followed the movements. Martha was watchful of every step and followed Edward's voice behind her. She peeped anxiously inside a few holes on the walls and behind the wooden bars cladding the sides. It was only after a few seconds that she realized Edward had stopped talking. When no other sound came as a suggestion of his presence, she turned towards him.

Edward stood frozen at a corner as if influenced by an external force, but only it was not. Edward had ceased all activity at his own will. He almost appeared like a sculpture, lifeless yet almost real. For a moment Martha grew panicky, she stumbled towards him.

"Mr. Woods!" she called him.

Edward stopped Martha signalling with his arm stretched towards her. He could not be interrupted.

It was finally happening, the long due. Edward felt the recognizable company, a familiar presence, and it shelled him with nostalgia. His expressions changed to one of grief.

"I recognized you .....Wesley, it's you...isn't it?"

His voice turned grim when he addressed his beloved pal, and yes, it was indeed Wesley. Martha stood shocked at a corner as she followed everything that transpired then. Edward's eyes were closed when they turned wet. It was the recollection of the past, loss of a beloved one, and Martha's heart too felt a part of that pain. He stood like a mannequin; his head tilted towards the sky like an angel, overwhelmed by grief, with prayers on his lips. Someone had rightly said; the past left without a closure always comes back to haunt you, and for Martha it stood like a vivid proof of the ageless saying.

"I am sorry, Wesley. I couldn't save you." These were his final words.

His eyes were rushing beneath the closed cover of his eyelids as if he were seeing some images.

Tranquillity passed his mourning expressions; Edward was releasing the guilt he had lived with all these years. And in the midst of Edward's final words and his return, suddenly an unknown force hit Martha's hand. Under the effect of that push, her fingers loosened and the piece of paper flew out of her grip.

Martha did not run after it when it flew in open, twirling inside air windings. It took rather a long route after which it was caught by an open window. The paper stuck open on the windowpane and a part of it got stained after soaking a few drops of water. That portion of the paper now lay darkened. But it was not a random stain, because under the highlight of moisture stood out two words amongst all the others.

Edward saw the whole leap. He advanced towards the window and as he proceeded, he knew he was about to get the sign he was looking for. He peeled the paper from its right top corner and flattened it on his palm. Edward stared at the two words that stood highlighted and he realized someone had answered to his call.

He raised his eyes at Martha and in a composed look of bewilderment, he said, "You have a basement, right?"

Bass ....meant = Basement

Basement was another unwelcoming host, just like many other rooms inside the Barcaldine. To Martha, it seemed full circle, returning to the spot from where it all started, the horrifying dream. Edward announced his next move.

"I'll attempt to read the energy imprints here."

"What does that mean?"

"Every space has bundles of energy stored in it, accumulated from the past and present. The memories of the past somehow get imprinted inside these energies and survive. I know how to tune into them; my psychic abilities will take me into this incognito passage to the past." Edward explained looking around the ceiling, evaluating the size of the basement.

"Does that mean we can see what happened in this house?" Martha said in disbelief.

"Yes, there is a possibility, and only if there are sufficient imprints."

"How do you know the energies are strong in here?"

"I don't know," he continued, "but we have been directed down here, so I owe it a chance."

Martha was hopeful. However, she desperately wanted David to be here. She decided if it didn't work, she would at least call him and ask him to join her as soon as possible.

"It must add to your bewilderment, Martha?" Edward added.

"A lot has lately. Now I am just abiding to whatever is coming my way."

Edward nodded in understanding.

"These energies are very subtle at times. We all have felt their impressions from time to time."

"How's that possible?"

Edward lowered down to look between the stacks at the corners of the lengthy wall. By feeling the roughness of the cloth covering them, and the lines on the floor, he assimilated the potential.

"Have you ever found yourself missing someone and going through their things just to feel close to them. I remember, whenever I missed my grandfather, I used to go through his clothes, smell them, and it felt as if he was just with me. There is this palpable energy of the person the object belongs to, and it's even more evident if that object is very dear to them," he explained.

Martha nodded. While he spoke, Edward felt a strange unrecognizable anxiety but couldn't put a finger on why. But the whole conversation with Martha somehow helped him to focus and he stuck to the conversation for a little longer.

"That is why I never buy old or vintage articles sold in auctions. Strange as it sounds, sometimes these inanimate objects can also act as mediums of travel for the spirits left behind. I might sound superstitious, but awareness makes you cautious."

"Does that mean the dead can follow us and stick around, is that the danger?"

"Quite possible. Visions of the past if they are reachable, or the spirit can manifest itself before the next owner of their possessions, which happens in very extreme conditions, and only if it is still hovering around, but, yes, possible if those objects were dear to them when they were alive."

As if the purpose of the additional talk was over, Edward without announcing his next move positioned himself before a wall. He spread his palms on its surface. He sharply closed his eyes and began to focus. His fingers trembled when it touched the rough surface of the wall and as he screened the length of the basement with his hands, he tried to sync his mind with the energy that he could feel. He felt every grain, the pinch of a hole at the upper end, and the sharp undulations. In between, he rubbed his fingertips as if sharpening their receptivity.

The movements were as steady as that of a painters' brush. Martha was curiously following the range of his gestures when suddenly his hands came to an abrupt halt. It was when Edward stopped at a particular portion of the wall, like a magnet sticking to iron. His eyebrows frowned and his head slightly bent to his left as if listening to something closely. Martha continued to play the role of the silent spectator for whom the anticipation of meeting the end of the night grew with every event. She needed no explanation this time, she knew what was happening; Edward was seeing images of a gone time. Finally, he was witnessing the unheard!

The images were gripping, Edward breathed sharply in surprise. His lips parted, speechless, but Edward didn't lose his hold over the past, a past which was unknown till now, waiting to be discovered inside the dark energies of Barcaldine.

Martha saw the end arriving. She trembled at the sight of the misty darkness in the cell. Yet, she kept obedient to her accomplice. The inside and outside of the Barcaldine had moved worlds apart. The truth was being transited through the mind of a house to that of a human.

And then it came...

Next what Martha heard was a painful scream. Not an ear outside was exposed to it, because the evil had begun its game inside the Barcaldine and was prepared to swallow its next victim. That cry was from no one else but Edward and when Martha realized it, he was already tumbling on his feet like he had suffered an electric shock. His body quivered. His face had gone pale as if someone had soaked the blood out of his veins. Martha ran to him, something beyond his control had happened.

"Martha – Martha!" he was gasping for air.

"Mr. Woods – what happ- what happened to you,"

"Mart – not them — oh lord, we have been tricked! It's not the one we have been thinking all along –" his words struggled through his hyperventilating lungs.

"What! What do you mean, Mr. Woods! Why are you so frightened?!"

He lay on his back and his strength seemed to have had drained out. His head had gone wet with sweat, his eyes wide with fear and shock.

"No, Martha we nee- need to get out! Now!" Edward shuffled his head furiously. He was losing his mind; his body was drained.

"Why, Mr. Woods, what did you see? What did you see?"

"We –need-to-get – it's never been the Willards talking to us!"

"What!!! What are you talking?"

Edward furiously shook his head in disagreement like a mad person and kept on repeating the same thing.

"We need to get out, lord we shouldn't have come!." He couldn't bring himself together to speak the rest of it.

"Who is it then!?" Martha screamed at him, and Edward finally revealed the truth to her.

"It's Emily! "Edward cried, "The adopted daughter of the Willards and she is buried right there!"

And with this, his trembling finger pointed at Emily's grave, pointing where her dead corpse was buried which was beneath the floor of the basement.

Suddenly, a loud deafening thump echoed. The floors shook and the walls shuddered. It left Martha petrified and she let out a ghastly cry. It was Edward who first got on his feet. He pulled Martha's hand and darted towards the door of the basement. There was nothing left to know and Martha realized they needed to get out of Barcaldine, now! The alarm had been set around them, the entities had been awakened, and Barcaldine was alive. And then followed another thump and a crack appeared on the wall.

The rush of the moment was as vivid as seen in the dream about the basement earlier. To Martha, it felt she had foreseen the future then, just like dejavu. Edward and Martha got out of the basement when they heard the wooden floor burst open behind them. A frightening change took over. In a matter of seconds, the house morphed into a living hell, as if every part of it had awakened its sleeping demon.

Destruction took over, like hit by an earthquake. From the corner of her eye, Martha saw something coming after them, something which had a shape and body, with life in it. Something which had appeared from the crack in the wall. Edward saw it too and the memory of how Paul was dragged by a figure who came from the wall hit him, leaving a sinking feeling in the pit of his stomach.

They reached the main staircase and the exit door was only a few meters away. Edward pulled Martha to overcome her failing feet, she did not know why but a tightening cramp had seized her.

"Martha, come!! There is no time!" Edward hastened and pushed Martha.

As if to delay their rescue, suddenly a beam from the top came falling down. It fell with a frightening speed and a deafening sound. Edward saw it. He pushed Martha and jumped away in time, escaping getting hit by the beam. They survived but unfortunately got separated, as now between them lay a massive immovable beam. Not only were they separated, the massive beam had blocked Martha's way to the exit, while for Edward it was still free.

Just then, Martha heard a howl from behind. It instantly shot the tension in her and the throbbing pain in her head. Every development came one after another, leaving no time to register any of it.

"Martha!!! Run!!," Edward screamed in terror from the other side when he saw the creature behind her.

Martha on the sudden call grabbed the staircase and ran upstairs. She ran without the slightest care where she was heading. Her legs paced mechanically and it felt she had no control over them anymore. Martha did not stop until she reached the second floor. She threw her heavy long coat on the stairs when its weight kept delaying her easy run. She ran crying, wailing, and gasping for air. She entered the second-floor hallway, continued to run, and reached the grand door of the assembly hall. Pushing it hard she entered inside the hall and closed the door behind. A mistake she had done, she had reached the farthest corner in the house from the only exit downstairs...

Martha sobbed uncontrollably; she looked pitiful. She felt a dread when she realized she had no way to escape now. Only months ago, she had nothing to do with

Barcaldine, and today, it stood tall to claim her life. She could hear the growls of the evil causing destruction on the lower floors. She panicked thinking about Edward; fearing if he had been taken away by the house too, or had he left grabbing his chance of an escape? Martha began to weep like a child holding her cross so tightly that its pointed edge caused blood to run from her fingers.

What was to happen next? There was not a hint of it, the night had gone wrong. Martha realized it was the end. End of her life, the night had gone terribly wrong!

She heard a buzzing sound. It was coming from someplace very near and then she felt vibrations on her left thigh, her phone was ringing that she had slid inside her jeans. A wishful hope resurfaced which felt like a blessing when she saw David's name flashing on the screen.

Martha hit the flap open.

"Hello! David –David!" she turned hysterical and broke into a pitiful sob hearing him on the other line. "Help me! David - help, help... Pleeasse... I am stuck!"

"Martha!! What happened!? Why are crying?!" an alarm set in his voice as he heard her panicky cries.

"David, please come back...." she gasped for air, "I am- I am stuck in the house, they'll kill me."

"What!? Oh my god! Where are you, Martha? What has happened! Who is there??"

Before Martha could say anything further, the door of the assembly hall jerked with a creepy strong push. It was so loud that the door shook inside its frame. The howling creature had finally reached her.

"NOOO!," Martha cried. David heard the noise too.

"OH lord, Martha! Martha! What was that? God! What is happening?!" these were his last words before the battery died.

The phone slipped from her hand and Martha's red bulging eyes were struck with terror when she saw the horror sliding on the wall.

A bulge appeared marking a noticeable long crack. And if this wasn't enough to scare Martha's very soul, the bulge began to crawl like a creepy lizard running for its prey. But the creature crawled inside the wall shrouding its identity. Reaching the wall opposite to hers, the bulge stopped right before Martha. The crack progressed into a complete tearing of the wooden planks and at last emerged the ferocious ghost of Emily, emerging out again after decades.

It had a face of child, but looked like the child of Satan, lacking those features that once made her look human. But it was enough for Martha to see the real face of Emily. Contrary to this, the body was of a large woman and oriented like that of an insect. It seemed as if vengeance fed her this devilish form. But vengeance for what? Martha still didn't know. Edward could not tell her.

When the ghost emerged out of the wall and fell on the floor, its movements progressed and produced a rapid rasping sound. Her arms seemed to be made of disoriented joints as she headed towards Martha to claim her.

Martha was left drenched in fear at the progress of that sneering figure. The ghost's head twisted to its sides like a mechanical neck of an insane patient. Martha sobbed uncontrollably. Her screams grew disturbing and reminded you of the ones heard in the dark chambers of asylums.

"NO... NO, please... leave me for god's sake...don't don't..."

Martha realized it was the end of everything and this was the last that she heard from David. But this was not the death she had imagined for herself, life seemed unfair even at the end. The faces of her kids flashed before her eyes, which she would never see again.

Martha did not want to die, but then who did? The end was here and nobody had seen death approaching so closely, visibly and evidently. A ghost was coming for her. It would just be a matter of minutes when Emily would prison her soul like she did with the Willards. But why Emily? Why was she the mystery and the evil of Barcaldine? Martha realized she would never know.

Martha cried mourning for her own end that was approaching with ticking time. Yes, her cries were mournful; seldom any human had been forced to cry his or her own death. Yes, she already felt dead; soon the breath running in her lungs would be snatched too.

Then in the whole havoc of life and death, evil and good... something happened!

Martha heard footsteps, the sound of which grew with every passing second. Someone was running up the stairs. Edward was coming for her. Martha realized and the last wishful hope in her resurfaced. But would he be able to reach her in time? The question still hovered like a knife against her throat.

The sound of those hasty steps reached the assembly hall and the door flew open. But it was not Edward as she thought; it was the most unexpected person; it was Amie! She was standing right in front of Martha at the door as she called for her.

"Martha, come out! Now!" Amie shouted alarmingly.

Martha's wishful hope pushed strength in her one last time at Amie's command. She regained the balance of her knees and beamed towards the door with a force alien to her.

The ghost howled after her, for losing its victim, and with that, the door shut itself to imprison Martha again. But

Martha managed to escape with Amie before the shutters smacked behind her.

The shaky earthquake returned and it felt the house would topple down any minute. Amie grabbed Martha's hand and ran. She had determination. She was her rescuer. Amie did not say a word and just advanced towards their escape. Martha ran along in full strength; nothing could stop her now. God had graced the last chance for life and Martha was not letting it go.

They finally reached the stairs and rushed down with firm feet. The ceiling groaned and the walls quivered, all under the anguish of the ghost that must be out again to catch them. When the front of the beam that ceased her exit reappeared, her eyes hastened for Edward. The beam had been slightly moved so they could run out. Who did that? It did not matter.

Martha reached the door and her urging eyes located Edward. He was lying unconscious at the entrance of the living room.

"Amie, wait! I have to take him with me – Mr. Woods!" Martha stopped.

"Martha, there's no time. You have to get out of here," Amie said.

"No, I can't without him," Martha protested further but Amie seemed determined.

"He will be taken care of," Amie said.

"What - what do you mean?"

Suddenly, Martha saw a boy, a young slouching figure wearing old jeans and a leather jacket. He was standing just beside Edward's unconscious body, staring at him with his head bent low. Amie without saying a word opened the main door and threw Martha out of the house. Martha felt shocked at Amie's persuasion. She was unable to get to

Edward as he lay far from her now, inside the house, being watched by another mysterious ghost of the past.

"No, Amie! I can't leave him," Martha shouted at her.

Martha got up to make her way in, but a beating force pushed her away, and just then she noticed something; Amie did not come out of the house and stood just at frame of the door.

"Go, Martha," said Amie.

"What?" Martha questioned shockingly.

"Yes, go...there is no time!" said Amie, softening this time.

"And – And what about you? I can't leave you behind; your family is worried for you."

"I can't, Martha... but you have to go now, before she comes and gets you," replied Amie.

"What are you saying!!!" cried Martha. She reached for Amie's hand. Amie pushed Martha away from her and she fell even farther from the entrance this time. When she got up to protest again, she witnessed something which nobody had seen in ages; it had happened for the first time, leaving Martha shocked and numb – she saw the whole Willard family, all the four members stood just behind Amie; she saw the son of the Willards for the first time, looking out at Martha with plain, hollow eyes.

"Yes, Martha," Amie bent her face solemnly, "I can't, I am one of them now. The house got me too." A grim tear fell from her eye.

Before Martha could react to the revelation, a tornado rushed out of the house, trapping Martha in it and throwing her further away from Barcaldine. And like a twin impact of that force, simultaneously Edward's body dashed out, crashing the window of the living room. She saw Edward come falling on the muddy grass after her and lying a few feet away from where she fell. They were being helped. With this, the doors of the Barcaldine twisted around the hinges and shut on their own, loudly against the broad frame. And that was the last sight of Amie ever seen by the living world.

Amie was dead and to Martha it felt no less than losing a close friend. The Barcaldine had finally revealed itself naked; a part to Edward and a part to her.

The rain continued relentlessly and Martha got up on her aching legs. Painful red scratches marked her arm that worsened when the soil burnt them further. She was panting hard but she managed to reach Edward. She quickly checked his pulse; he was still alive. But time was running. They had to get out of Barcaldine's territory; the final countdown had begun.

She tried to wake Edward, but he lay unconscious. Martha was now alone in this final act of their rescue, getting to the main gate seven meters away, and setting them both free from the danger that still clouded their fate.

Martha began to drag Edward's body. The wet soil caused friction but she struggled against it. She owed it to Edward, and to Amie. Martha grabbed him by both hands, dragging him behind her. The fear of the whole night had not subsided. She somehow covered a few meters. Her muscles were aching under the freezing rain and numbness began to envelope her skin. But she pushed and covered more distance.

The gate finally stood two meters away now and its lock was open. Martha calculated that she could straightaway barge into the gates without halting to unlock it. Freedom was almost near and soon they will be out. Her heart already began to celebrate the victory. But it was too soon to rejoice yet, the evil was still after them.

When Martha turned once to look at Barcaldine, suddenly the same bulge appeared again on the ground. It instantly grew large and came rushing towards them with alarming speed. Martha screamed with all her lungs at the sight of it. Emily had again appeared with greater strength.

"NO NO NO...!" Martha began to shriek as the bulge grew bigger and closer.

Martha was a few steps away from her freedom and the ghost was advancing at an alarming speed. The fear froze her. She began to thump Edward's chest hoping to wake him up. She was losing control over her muscles. Her shaking body had no strength left to drag him further.

"Wake up! Wake up!" Martha cried in the dark night.

Martha still pushed herself, took another step or two, and her skin almost touched the cold metal of the gate. But alas, her body froze right at the face of her ultimate escape.

Freedom was just a push away and the ghost, two meters from catching them. Martha panicked and shrieked. Warm sweat pinched her skin even in the cold night. Finally, the rotten hand emerged out from the mud, right before Martha's eyes. It would now take only a few more seconds for the hand to grab and get hold of her. She shut her eyes. A defeating sorrow hit her and she finally gave up. She could almost smell death closer as Emily was just a moment away from claiming her victims.

Martha remembered her family and God for the last time, the battle had ended for Martha and in her mind, Emily had won.

And then again, luck held her hand, like before.

Suddenly, Martha fell forward under immense weight. The force barged her out of the iron gate and with that the freedom was declared. Edward had gotten on his feet in time. He jumped at Martha, pushing both of them free from the boundaries of Barcaldine.

The ghost touched the gate, howled, and vanished at the periphery of the Barcaldine territory.

Finally, the struggle of the night reached its due end!

Martha and Edward without wasting a moment further geared the car and drove far away from the horrendous smell of Barcaldine, swearing never to return.

Edward turned at Martha, exchanged a plain look of shock to what all they just witnessed, and set the car moving on the dark silent lanes of Lanthom Cove.

***

Martha called David from the phone in the car and when she met him three hours later near the town's entrance, she hugged him tightly, and sobbed for hours as if Emily still could steal her away from him.

CHAPTER TWENTY-SIX

A journey ends, another begins, and that is the course of life. Maybe Martha was destined to experience some peculiar hardships, even the ones fought by warriors of good and evil.

Edments stayed for two days at the Woods Residency. The decision to return back to New York was then duly taken. David recalled the urgency in Martha's voice when she was trapped in the house, he did not demand any other explanation. He could have lost Martha and it still disturbs him.

David believed every word Edward said, when he revealed what he saw that night. Emily Willard did not disappear in the woods, did not get lost or got killed by some animal; Emily was murdered by her own blood. Edward saw clear images of Mr. and Mrs. Willard strangling the innocent girl while she pleaded for life. They stabbed her mercilessly till she lost the last stroke of breath. It was a bloody vision; a corpse of an innocent girl drenched in blood getting dragged into the basement. To hide their sins, Willards cleanly buried her body under the basement and sealed her tomb in the house itself. Another unknown man, whose identity Edward could not decipher, was an accomplice in this crime.

Contrary to the narrative known to the world, the Willards, instead of feeling love and acceptance for Emily, loathed her, and that hatred was so spiteful, that even their conscience could not counter the sinful decision of murdering Emily. She was a burden to them, an unnecessary expense, and a possible roadblock for Mr. Willard in inheriting his dead brother's estate.

Edward's faith in his visions revealed the beginning of the misery, from where it all started. The tale of cruelty did not end with Emily's death; it turned into a spiral of vengeance. Emily returned, her mourning soul possessed the Willards and made their deaths seem like tragedies. Edward witnessed all the visions of the past. Mr. Willard jumped from the window in sleep; it wasn't suicide. The insanity of Mrs. Willard was also the result of Emily's terror and possession followed by killings of her innocent cousins. Emily, who now was the shadow of evil herself, prisoned these souls inside the house with her, just like what they did to her. May be that was the reason behind the fear in the eyes of the girl who Martha saw in the basement. Martha remembered that face, which wasn't of Emily but must be of the daughter of Mr. and Mrs. Willard.

Martha had finally witnessed the unheard of Barcaldine, but who really was the unheard amongst all of them – was it Emily who in her   rage did not even spare her innocent cousins? or were they Mr. and Mrs. Willard who wanted to admit their sinful crime and set themselves free from the burden of lie and cruelty? Or were they the Willard's children who paid heavily for the sinful deeds of their parents? Some things we can never know, even when they stand clear like an open book. After all, memories are also victims of time.

Another tale woven by human greed, hatred, and cruelty resulted into a gruesome murder. Martha's dream house now stood as one of the many bearers of the evils carried by men, tainted by time, and suffered by the innocents. But why Martha had to come across Barcaldine to be the voice of its gruesome past, why she? Maybe it was destiny too.

For a few consecutive nights, Martha, at unrest, wondered the reason behind Emily's death. Was it greed, hatred or just baseless loathing? The tale was not new, many innocent lives have been slaughtered before for the same baseless loathing, but for Martha, this story had become the dent of her life. This time her core witnessed the extent of inhumanity humans could go to. Emily wasn't the real evil here but the very basic emotions like jealously, hatred, and ego.

Today is Martha's last day in Lanthom Cove. The cursed Barcaldine is having its space emptied, beginning another era of deep silence, bound to continue its lonesome journey.

Martha stood outside the boundary of the house beside the car, watching their material possessions getting loaded into the trucks. Someone had said wisely; to be free of fear, one has to face it. Martha faced Barcaldine and it had no more power over her now, her eyes displayed no emotion for it.

The destruction caused inside the house was told to be the result of its weakened structure; no one questioned further. Ben and Susan will also never know the truth.

A man came out carrying the coat Martha left on the stairs during the struggle of the night. He approached her, "Mrs. Edment, I guess this is yours," the man said and offered her the coat.

"Yes, it is mine," she replied calmly in a low voice. "Thank you." She had her eyes lowered.

"This looks expensive, keep it safe," he said smiling.

"Yes, I would remember that," she replied. She was not offended nor was it meant to be. Her mind was not really responding to the trivial matters of the world anymore. Her experience had induced a new perspective in her.

In the next few minutes, she will be out of the town forever, back to the city where her life actually began. Martha wondered why and how Amie died. It seemed that the memory of Barcaldine was still left unheard with this last unsolved piece of the puzzle. Then it crossed Martha that may be some things are better left unheard; Amie unfortunately was to be one such mystery.

Martha gave a final glance at the house. The time she had spent there can never be reversed, neither will she ever forget the dent it had caused. But yes, she was leaving the wounds behind. She decided she could not move on being a victim of Barcaldine. She gave a look of victory towards the house, telling it that even though it played with her life, she won. In the end, it is the one getting abandoned again like always. She pitied the house for its fate. Martha decided to put an end to this vicious game of Barcaldine and she knew there was only one way to do it.

Martha brushed the long coat and wore it to protect herself from the cold breeze. She walked to Edward who was standing near the side of the road, reviewing his life from the day it all began in 1976 till today. Again, Barcaldine marked beginning of another phase in Edward's life, but this time it was one of accomplishment. He could now finally move on from the haunting of his past.

Martha went and hugged him heartily; she felt the fatherly touch in his hug. Their lives were meant to cross through Barcaldine only to bond forever.

Saying her goodbye, Martha sat inside the car leaving everything behind.

She drove off with her family and with Barcaldine sliding behind them through the view of the car window.

***

She recalled the route, the hill, the river, and the clouds above, all the same since the first day of her arrival. David caressed her hand as they drove out of the boundaries of the town. Martha smiled at the gesture and slid her hand into the pockets of her coat. It was then when she found something inside her coat. She felt its edges; hard, and its weight thin. She took it out; it was a card like paper folded onto its one side. The edges were yellow and its back cramped and wrinkled.

"What is it?" David asked.

"I don't know," she replied.

Martha unfolded it. It was a photograph, a very old photograph, black and white in print.

There were five people standing in it and she recognized each one of them; it was the entire Willard family in one frame. Every figure standing firm with faces sourly plain as if sculpted. She recognized everyone, including Emily.

She demanded from David to stop the car and then got out. David couldn't understand when she asked for his lighter. What caused her to burn the photograph? It was not the scare of seeing the Willards again, but that something which solved the last piece of the whole Barcaldine puzzle.

As David saw the edge of the old photograph catch fire, he asked in a calm-curious voice, "What did you see, Martha?"

Yes, she saw something, which Emily was wearing. When Martha did not respond, David questioned again, "What was it?"

She answered emotionlessly, "I saw a pearl pendant." But it was not just any pearl pendant; it was the one that

Amie had around her neck. It did not take Martha much time to bring everything together – Amie's grandfather worked for the Willards, there was an unknown accomplice while the Willards killed Emily, and the talk that Edward made about objects becoming a medium of travel for the evil spirits sealed everything together. Amie wore it all the time. Martha did not have to know what Amie thought were hallucinations in her early days, were in fact Emily's spirit following her like a shadow, through the pendant.

David did not question her further as the last document of the Willard family turned into restless ashes before his eyes.

"David, let's go," Martha said.

With that, the car drove off to continue its journey and only halted once they were back in New York.

Two days after the Edment family departed from Barcaldine, the resolute decision to demolish the house was made by Mrs. Edment herself, a choice that nobody questioned. The fate of the decomposed corpse discovered in the basement was then decided. It underwent examination, revealing it to be decades old.

Once the necessary investigations were completed, the remains were respectfully cremated, closing the circle of life and death that had cursed the life of Barcaldine, and eventually lead to its demise too.

***END

AVENUE OF DEATH

An old university, a haunting past, and the one who
will discover it, is arriving.
Because; *her beginning was its end...*
Releasing in 2026

Akash Bansal writing as Ash Banss
Follow him on Insta and stay connected for
updates @writerakashbansal

Also By Akash Bansal

Set in Tuscany, Her Last Walk is a tale of soulmates and witchcraft. A woman after losing the love of her life to death meets a wiccan witch who tells her about a magical path to reunite with her lost love.